DEATH TAKES A HOLIDAY

COUNTRY COTTAGE MYSTERIES 18

ADDISON MOORE
BELLAMY BLOOM

The Country Cottage Inn is known for its hospitality. Leaving can be murder.

My name is Bizzy Baker, and I can read minds. Not every mind, not every *time*, but most of the time, and believe me when I say, it's not all it's cracked up to be.

The summer heat is pressing down on Cider Cove as Bizzy's relatives descend on the inn for a family reunion. But not everyone is thrilled to see one another. Bizzy's mother, Ree, is forced to confront her estranged sisters and the man that came between them all those years ago. And when that man turns up dead, there are one too many suspects—and three of them happen to be sisters. Summer in Cider Cove is proving to be deadly.

Bizzy Baker runs the Country Cottage Inn, has the ability to pry into the darkest recesses of both the human and animal mind, and has just stumbled upon a body. With the help of her kitten, *Fish*, a mutt named Sherlock Bones, and an ornery yet dangerously good-looking homicide detective, Bizzy is determined to find the killer.

Cider Cove, Maine is the premier destination for fun and relaxation. But when a body turns up, it's the premier destination for murder.

CHAPTER 1

"Welcome to the Pahrump Family Reunion," my mother says, lacking the proper enthusiasm one might have for such a familial bonding experience.

It's August. The sun is bearing down on Cider Cove, on all of *Maine*. It's hot and muggy, and it feels as if that ball of fire in the sky is being strained through a wet blanket.

Since my extended family was looking for a location to host its annual shindig, I volunteered the Country Cottage

Inn, the resort I inherited through a rather horrific event last winter. But despite the morbid way I came to own the place, the inn has been my baby for over half a decade. That's exactly how long I've been managing the place.

The inn is an ivy-covered cobblestone structure that happens to butt up against a sandy cove along the picturesque Maine coastline. The cove is an expansive wonder with rocky crags on one end and a wall of evergreens on the other. Behind the woods, there's a bluff with a gazebo sitting on it. And in front of that, the rocky shoreline trickles to meet the sand.

The beach is teeming with guests this afternoon, but I've cordoned off a small area where the Pahrumps can enjoy their reunion uninterrupted. Some of my relatives flew in from afar, but most live within driving distance to Cider Cove, so having it at the inn this year just made sense.

Soothing music floats from the speakers set up next to the grills that are cooking up our feast, and the scent of barbequed burgers and hot dogs permeates the air. My Aunt Birdie owns a bistro up in Brambleberry Bay and wanted to contribute to the festivities, so she brought along all of the side dishes, including dessert.

I had my groundskeeper, Jordy Crosby, set up dozens of picnic tables with umbrellas so there will be more than enough seating for everyone. Who knew there were close to seventy Pahrumps who would be present and accounted for today? Somewhere out here I have cousins that I haven't seen in ages. I was hardly seven when I saw them last. I don't think I stand a chance recognizing anyone in the wild today. I had one cousin named Hattie who was my exact same age, and we did everything together until my mother yanked her family out from under us like a rug she thought no longer went with the decor. They weren't getting along too well in the first place, but I sure missed them.

A hairy man in a pair of Speedo swim trunks strides by and Georgie groans as if she were mortally wounded.

"Hubba hubba," she says low and throaty.

Georgie Conner is a kaftan-loving eighty-something-year-old woman with gray wiry hair and a smidge of mischief in her lavender-blue eyes. She's an artist who specializes in mosaics, but she recently opened up a quilt shop with my mother called Two Old Broads.

"Down, girl," my mother tells her. Mom is a petite woman whose caramel-colored hair is forever feathered and shellacked à la 1980-something. She's donned a pink and white gingham top with the collar popped up near her ears for the occasion—another ode to her favorite decade—and a pair of white capri pants that I wouldn't be brave enough to wear to the library, let alone a cookout. "You're going to meet a lot of my relatives today, Georgie. And almost all of them have brought their husbands, wives, boyfriends, girlfriends, and children. I'm going to have family up the wazoo. The last thing I need is drama. And since I'm smart enough to know there will be drama, I'm also smart enough to say we're not getting involved in any of it. All men are off-limits to you this weekend. If I could survive without a man for the last fifteen years, you can last two days."

Georgie grunts in response, "Says the one with the hot boyfriend with the Scottish accent."

It's true. As of a couple of months ago, my mother is very much taken by a Scottish hunk named Brennan Gallagher. In fact, I see him now in line at the bar.

Brennan is a perfect gentleman. I couldn't have picked anyone better for her. I mean, my father is pretty great himself, but his weakness for other women put the kibosh on their legal union. That's how I met Georgie. Her daughter, Juniper Moonbeam—*Juni*—was my father's fifth or fifteenth bride. I can never keep them straight. I like to tease that I got Georgie in the divorce.

"There they are," my mother growls at a group of women crouching in the shade of an evergreen. "My *sisters*." She spits the word *sisters* out as if it were an expletive. And considering the fact she's done her best to avoid her sisters for as long as I can remember, it might as well have been. Two of the women are her sisters indeed, the other two I can't quite identify.

Personally, I'm surprised my mother can identify anyone here. My mother hasn't been to a family reunion in years. So when my Aunt Birdie told me that their regular venue had shut down and asked if I could host it, I couldn't say no. My mother wasn't too thrilled with the news.

"Aw, come on, Preppy." Georgie threads her arm through my mother's. "Your boyfriend is getting the booze, and I'm packing heat under this kaftan. If one of those girls gets testy, we've got you covered."

"Georgie, please tell me you didn't bring Thor," I say.

Thor is the name of the handgun she purchased from a pawn shop a while back, and that bad boy has been nothing but trouble ever since.

"Nah, I'm just burning up," she says, pulling off her hot pink kaftan in a single maneuver and treating us to more lightning white wrinkles than the human eye should have to endure. She's got on a red bikini that sags up top and disappears intermittently beneath folds of flesh down below. "You're welcome," she shouts at a group of men ogling her from afar. "Now let's go show those sisters of yours what we've got."

A spray of sand kicks up nearby and we turn to see my sweet cat and perky pup, Fish and Sherlock Bones, heading this way.

Fish mewls as she practically jumps into my arms, *There are ornery beasts all over this beach today, Bizzy. Why do people bring their dogs everywhere they go and yet you hardly see cats?*

Sherlock gives a few quick barks. *Because we're easier for people to deal with.*

That's because you can be hypnotized by bacon. Fish gives a mild swipe his way. *It takes a lot more to sway my kind. We're not some silly robots who can be programmed to do whatever people like by way of salty meat.*

A tiny laugh brews in my chest at the thought. She's not wrong. I could get Sherlock to dance a jig all across the shoreline at the mention of bacon.

I give my sweet cat a quick scratch.

Fish is a black and white long-haired tabby who I found a few years back. She's as witty and wise as she is cute. And Sherlock Bones is a red and white freckled mutt who once belonged to Homicide Detective Jasper Wilder, but lucky for me, both Sherlock Bones and Jasper belong to me now.

My name is Bizzy Baker *Wilder*, and I can read minds. Not every mind, not every time, but it happens, and believe me, it's not all it's cracked up to be—with the exception of conversations like these. Yes, I can read the animal mind, too, and they almost always have better things to say than humans. And I'm not sure how, but the animals seem to understand each other, and nothing thrills me more.

I drop a kiss to Fish's furry forehead. "You two might want to get along. We're about to see family we haven't spoken to in years." I nod at Georgie. "My mother has two sisters, my Aunt

Birdie and my Aunt Ruth. Mom used to be hot and heavy with some football player back in college named Glenn Pitts. And right around the time Mom thought he was about to propose, Aunt Ruth snatched him out from under her."

"That's right." Mom scoffs. "And then Birdie came along and snatched him from under Ruth. The Pahrump sisters haven't been the same ever since."

Fish yowls up at me, *If we're lucky, Macy might snatch Jasper away from you, and he'll move out and take Sherlock with him.*

I frown at her for even suggesting it. My sister, Macy, is a man-eater who goes through the opposite gender like a pack of potato chips. But thankfully, Jasper only has eyes for me, so I know for a fact that little scenario isn't playing out in the near or distant future.

We head over to the dubious women in question. My aunts stand to one side as a pretty brunette in a gauzy blue dress stands just shy of them, and in front of my aunts is a redhead with a pair of bright yellow sunglasses on.

Aunt Birdie looks the same as she did when I last saw her over twenty years ago when I was just about seven. She's petite with blonde hair and has big doe eyes and lips that take up most of her face. She looks to be every bit the saucy firecracker I remember in that red sleeveless shirt paired with denim short-shorts that my mother wouldn't be caught dead in.

Aunt Birdie takes a moment to gasp at the sight of my mother before reverting her attention to the redhead in yellow sunglasses.

"You tell that louse he's got a lot of nerve," Aunt Birdie shouts at the woman. *And the nerve of him showing up looking like a dream. He knows I can't resist him in turquoise swim shorts. Glenn Pitts is going to pay for this. And I'm going to personally dole out the punishment.*

"Louse?" The redhead scowls right back. "He thinks the same of you." *He's a louse, all right, for dragging me out here to begin with.* She stomps off and the tension only ticks up a notch once she leaves.

Standing next to Aunt Birdie is another blonde with vanilla waves and bowtie lips that keep twitching side to side as if she doesn't know whether to laugh or cry. That's my Aunt Ruth. I recognize her, too. And next to Aunt Ruth is a young woman about my age with dark hair and pretty green eyes with a hint of dimples on either of her cheeks. She's gorgeous, but her beauty is eclipsed by that stunning tan tabby she's holding in her arms who looks to be smiling over at Fish.

Finally. Another reasonable creature, the tiny tabby mewls. *And to think I thought I was going to have to endure the barking brigade all weekend.*

Sherlock gives a soft woof up at her. *Watch it, whiskers. I happen to belong to the barking brigade myself.*

"Well, well, if it isn't the third Pahrump sister." Aunt Ruth forces a smile. "I guess we are seeing you again *over your dead body.*"

"She doesn't look dead to me." Aunt Birdie dives over my mother and gives her a tight embrace.

"There's always hope," Aunt Ruth mutters while Aunt Birdie waves her off.

"Don't listen to her, Ree." Aunt Birdie steps back. "We're not here to kill you. In fact, we never should have let a man get between us. Look at you two ninnies. I'm the one who stole both of your boyfriends—and, ironically, I get along the best with the two of you."

"That's because *she* stole him first." Mom points an accusatory finger at Aunt Ruth.

Aunt Ruth tosses up her hands. "And I told you a million times, I didn't steal him. I thought he was cheating on *me* with *you*." Her voice hikes up a notch, and it becomes crystal clear this situation is less *old bygone* and more *open wound*.

Aunt Birdie snorts. "We should band together and kill him. That oughta make all of us feel a little better. We can be the murder squad."

"Murder squad!" Georgie bucks with laughter. "I like your sisters, Preppy," she says, patting my mother on the back. "And here I thought they'd be just as stuffy as you are. Little did I know I've been dealing with the fuddy-duddy Pahrump sister all along. Well, I've got news for you ladies." She hitches a thumb my way. "This one has a leg up in the murder squad department. I'd play nice with her, if you know what I mean. Some kids collect stamps, she collects corpses."

"Not true," I say. "I'm so glad to see you ladies. I'm Bizzy."

"*Bizzy!*" they shout at once as they explode over me with joyous hugs.

"You're so *big*," Aunt Birdie cries.

"And so *beautiful*," Aunt Ruth coos. "Bizzy, you remember Hattie. She's twenty-seven, just like you. You were babies the last time you were together." She holds a hand out to the brunette in the gauzy blue dress and my mouth falls open. "Hattie has been coordinating the reunion for years. No one makes things happen like this girl."

"Hattie?" I say in disbelief as I look at the stunning brunette with bright green eyes and dimples, and then it all comes back to me. "I'm so sorry! I didn't recognize you. In my mind's eye, my little cousin Hattie is still a cute seven-year-old in pigtails. It's so great to see you."

She laughs as we give one another a tight embrace.

"It's great to see you, too," she beams as she takes me in.

Fish Baker, my sweet cat mewls at the tabby in her arms.

Fish Baker Wilder, Sherlock Bones corrects with a bark. *Fish just hates the fact Bizzy found someone better to spend her time with—my dad, Jasper. He's a detective, and he catches the bad guys.*

Fish mewls once again, *Don't listen to him.* **Bizzy catches the bad guys. Jasper just shows up to arrest them.**

That's why they make a great team. Sherlock wags his tail and Hattie laughs as she gives him a quick scratch. *What's your name?* Sherlock barks as he touches the tabby's tail with his nose.

My name is Cricket and this is my mom, Hattie. She's special, too. She can hear your thoughts and understand what you're saying.

A breath hitches in my throat as I look at my cousin.

Hattie, can you hear me? I ask in disbelief.

Hattie's glowing green eyes squint as she smiles. *I sure can. In fact, I can hear just about everyone's thoughts. But I bet you can't hear me.* She winks along with the thought.

Oh, Hattie. I can't take my eyes off her. *I can hear you loud and clear.*

CHAPTER 2

"*Hattie*," I practically hiss her name out as I navigate her off to the side.

"*Bizzy Baker*," she hisses right back. "Can you really hear my thoughts?"

"It's Bizzy Baker Wilder." I wrinkle my nose. "I got hitched last year. And yes, I could hear everything you and your sweet cat were thinking—along with the rest of society, at least for the most part."

10

Both Fish and Cricket jump out of our arms and onto the sand before Sherlock begins to chase them around the cove.

Her mouth rounds out in a smile. "So do you know you're transmundane?"

A laugh bubbles from me. "Further classified as telesensual? How did you know about that?"

I had only recently learned about the transmundane community through Jasper's best friend, Leo Granger. They work at the Seaview Sheriff's Department together. And actually, Leo isn't working anywhere for the next two weeks. He's on his honeymoon with my best friend Emmie—technically, their *third or fourth* honeymoon, but that's a long story. A new truck and a curse are loosely involved. Having my best friend fall in love with Jasper's best friend has made me twice as happy for both of them—and us. They took their dogs, Cinnamon and Gatsby, along on their honeymoon do-over, and I miss their pooches as much as I miss them.

Hattie twitches a smile and her dimples dig in deep. "My grandmother—*our* grandmother—told me all about it before she passed away. I must have been eight at the time when she caught on that I was reading her thoughts. There's no doubt it's genetic. I guess she didn't know you had it, too."

"I wish I knew her better. I wish I knew all of the Pahrumps better. I can't believe my mother let a man stand in the way of family."

"*Both* of our mothers did the exact same rotten thing." She nods. "See that crowd under that blue and white striped umbrella?" She points about twenty feet out near the waterline where my sister Macy, my brother Huxley, and his wife Mackenzie chat along with two other women and a man. "Those are my siblings, and I just heard your thought, so I guess they're speaking with yours. None of my siblings share our gift, and believe me, I've tested the waters thoroughly." Her lips invert a moment. "No one else in my family knows about my gift. It's been my best-kept secret up until today."

"Wow," I say, squinting to inspect them. "I would never have recognized them in a million years."

"That's them. We're all still right up the coast in Brambleberry Bay. The guy with the dark wavy hair is my brother Henry. I don't know if you remember, but he's older than me. He's an attorney now, and he puts the shark in *shark*. The brunette with the pink dress is my older sister Winifred, but we still call her Winnie. She owns a craft shop and loves the beach. She's the one who suggested to Aunt Birdie we try your inn. The leggy blonde is my younger sister Cornelia—Neelie. She's a hurricane in a teapot. Trouble seems to follow her everywhere. She scored a job with our new hot mayor. Winnie is taking bets to see how long that lasts. And I'm an unemployed librarian. The branch where I worked made some cutbacks, and I was one of them."

"I'm sorry to hear it. I'm sure something new will come up. And who knows? It might even bring its own adventure."

"Here's hoping." She nods back toward our collective siblings. "So tell me about Macy and Huxley. It's been forever. Are they telesensual, too?"

"No. And much like you, I've tested those waters—so much so I'd be dead by now if they knew the thoughts I was slinging their way to see if they would respond. They don't know anything about my gift—if you can call it a gift." We share a knowing look. "Macy is still as boy crazy as ever. She owns a soap and candle shop right here on Main Street." I point up the way since the inn sits at the very edge of Main Street itself. "And Huxley is an attorney, too. I don't think we'll be able to separate him and Henry this weekend. That's his wife next to him. Mackenzie Woods is not only eight months pregnant with their baby, but she's the acting mayor of Cider Cove. Heads-up—she's a pistol."

A shaggy dog runs up with sandy blond fur. Its bangs are comically sitting on top of its head in a ponytail and it has a pair of sunglasses hanging from its neck.

They're arguing again. She barks in a distinctive light, female voice. *Oh, I can't stand the arguing. Can anyone help? I can't get them to stop. They're going to kill each other one of these days.*

"I'm on it," Hattie says, giving the furry pooch a quick pat. "Bizzy, this is Muffin. She's Uncle Glenn's Lhasa Apso. He said he needed a woman in his life after he and Aunt Birdie split a while back. They're actually in the middle of a messy divorce, but he really does consider this family as much his as it is hers. Come on, let's see if we can fix this disaster before it gets out of hand."

Muffin leads us over to the refreshment table where an entire line of glass footed bowls hold an ample amount of banana pudding.

A moan works its way up my throat.

Oh, just looking at the whipped cream and those delicious Nilla Wafers ensconced in mounds of vanilla pudding is making me want to dive right into one of those bowls.

But standing between me and my banana pudding dreams are Aunt Birdie and Uncle Glenn. My uncle is a chubbier, balder version of himself than I remember. He's donned a white tank top and glowing turquoise shorts, both of which look as if he's outgrown them by a belly-busting mile.

He and my aunt are having it out right here for all to see. Salty words are flying, causing every mother within earshot to whisk her young off in the opposite direction. A small crowd has amassed around us as they take in the free entertainment and a few people have their phones pointed this way so they can relive the moment at their leisure.

"Whoa, whoa," I say as I step their way, but my mother pulls me back.

"Oh no, you don't, Bizzy," she says. "Remember what I said? We're not getting involved in any family drama."

"Don't be silly. I'll be breaking it up." I try to take another step and Georgie pulls me back this time.

"They're just getting to the juicy part, Biz," Georgie snips. "Birdie accused him of having an affair, and Glenn's face turned into a turnip. I think he's going to explode into tiny bits of vegetable confetti."

Hattie beats me to the punch and quickly breaks up the carnage by asking them to stop or leave the premises if they can't behave.

I knew I liked her.

"Fine by me." Uncle Glenn tosses his hands in the air. "I never wanted to argue in the first place. Ask any Pahrump sister here. I'm a lover, not a fighter." He glances our way before doing a double take, and both my mother and Aunt Ruth groan because they know what's coming next.

Great. Aunt Ruth sighs hard. *He's spotted us. I don't suppose there's still time to get schnockered. I was hoping I'd have six drinks in me at least before I had to deal with his obnoxious smirk once again.*

Mom shakes her head. *Where is Brennan with those drinks, anyway? I need something strong and stiff, times six.*

Hattie chuckles to herself as she looks my way. *For being apart for so long, they sure think alike.*

I give a sly wink because she's right.

"Well, lookie here." Uncle Glenn's eyes widen with delight

as he heads our way. "If it isn't my two favorite Pahrump sisters, Ree and Ruthie." He ticks his head to the side as if reliving better times. "*Mmm, mmm,* how I've missed you. Ree, you haven't aged a day. And Ruthie, you look like a doll yourself." He lifts a brow to Georgie. "And hello to you, my golden lotus." His eyes ride up and down her bikini-clad body and he belts out a whistle.

"Oh, for goodness' sake." Mom shakes her head. "Bizzy, toss the cad out on his ear."

He looks my way, amused. "Little Bizzy? Ho, ho, ho!" He morphs into Santa. "Why, you're all grown up just like your cousin Hattie. And what a couple of cuties the two of you have turned out to be."

Muffin leaps forward and barks up at him. ***Thank goodness. You're on your best behavior. And you should stay on it, too. You and I both know these women have it out for you.*** Muffin looks back at Hattie. ***He told me so himself this morning.***

"It's nice seeing you again, Uncle Glenn," I tell him.

I don't have the heart to boot anyone out of the family reunion. Besides, it's not like I own the beach.

Georgie steps up to him. "Hey there, Hot Stuff. I won't give you any trouble unless trouble is what you're after." She gives a hard wink his way, and Mom groans.

"Oh please, Georgie." Mom shakes her head. "Your middle name is Trouble. Now back away from him before you spontaneously combust. The man is wicked to the core."

"Pay no mind to any of my exes," Uncle Glenn says, picking up Georgie's hand and kissing it. "In fact, swing by the Pitts Stop Dealership out in Edison sometime this week and I'll be sure to send you home in a beautiful car. A beautiful woman like you belongs in a beautiful set of wheels."

That's right. I remember hearing something about him and Aunt Birdie owning a car dealership.

I'm about to ask about it when a tall, dark, and dangerously handsome man in a suit pops up next to me and lands a kiss to my cheek.

"Everyone"—I call out—"this is my husband, Homicide Detective Jasper Wilder." I threw in that homicide bit just in case the murder squad decided this was a good time to cut their teeth on their first victim—aka Uncle Glenn.

The small crowd around us *oohs* and *ahhs*.

"Nice to meet you all." Jasper waves to those who've gathered. "I had to pop into the office for a few minutes today, so excuse the attire," he says.

"Homicide detective?" Uncle Glenn lifts a brow. "Well then. You might want to pay attention, son. One of these women is liable to plunge a knife into my back."

A titter of laughter circles around us.

Jasper nods to Uncle Glenn. "In that case, I'll keep an extra eye on you."

Our little crew disbands, and I navigate Jasper toward the bright-eyed brunette who happens to share my supernatural quirk.

"Jasper, this is my cousin Hattie. You're never going to believe this, but she's telesensual, too!" I can hardly hide my enthusiasm. Hattie and I had a special bond between us when we were kids, and now I wonder if this is why.

"No kidding?" he practically whispers as he holds out his hand and she shakes it. "It's a pleasure to meet you."

"You as well," she says. "You have no idea how glad I am to have reconnected with Bizzy, but to know that she's telesensual is the icing on the cake. Are you telesensual?"

"Not me." Jasper shakes his head emphatically. "My good

friend Leo is. He's on his honeymoon right now. And don't worry. Your secret is safe with me. I won't say a word."

I nod. "I won't either. Only a small handful of people are in on my secret. And here on the cove today it's just Jasper and Georgie who know. She's the one that called Uncle Glenn Hot Stuff."

Hattie chuckles. "She's a hoot, I can tell."

"Did the bathing suit give it away?" I tease. "Or was it the murder squad?"

Her mouth opens to say something, but her attention is hijacked by something near the rocky crags and I turn to find Uncle Glenn arguing with a bald man with a dark beard, wearing a dress shirt with a bowtie.

"I'm sorry," she says. "It's just that it looks as if they're about to come to blows."

"I'll take care of it," Jasper says. "And then, I'll run back to the cottage and do a quick change." He lands a kiss to my lips before jogging toward my poor uncle.

"Let's get a drink," I say to Hattie, and we head to the refreshment table, each grabbing a tall glass of strawberry lemonade.

"So are the rumors true?" she asks. "Do you really own this inn?"

"I sure do. The wealthy earl who I worked for passed away last Christmas and left it to me in his will." I leave out the part about him being murdered.

"Murdered?" She gasps as she looks right at me.

"*Ooh.*" I wince. "I'm actually going to have to get used to you reading my thoughts."

"Same here."

She does a double take toward the waterline. "Boy, Uncle Glenn is busy today."

17

I look that way to see him shouting something at that redhead with the yellow sunglasses I saw earlier. The same woman Aunt Birdie was telling off.

"He seems pretty steamed at her," Hattie says. "She probably turned down his proposition flat. Mom says he's a notorious flirt."

"Much to his detriment," I add.

Hattie and I chat about this and that, and it turns out, we have so much in common, from our shared love of books and animals to the way we take our lattes.

"I can't believe we lost all these years of getting to know one another all because of our mothers," I lament.

"Think of the shenanigans we could have gotten into."

I laugh at the thought just as I spot a man with long flowing hair, saying something curt to Uncle Glenn as the two of them head toward the woods.

"He's at it again," I say, and Hattie looks that way.

"That man is a magnet for trouble, I tell you. Rivaled only by my sister Neelie."

"Or my sister Macy," I say. "But she'd disagree and say that the true magnet for trouble would be me. Come on, let's dive into that banana pudding and I'll tell you all about the trouble I've seen."

Both Hattie and I help ourselves to a giant scoop of Aunt Birdie's luscious treat while I tell Hattie all about the bodies I've stumbled upon these past few years.

"No kidding?" She shakes her head as we make our way around the buffet table. "How is that even possible?"

"I don't know. I ask myself that every time I stumble upon another body. I'm just glad each case has been solved."

Wild barking catches our attention as Muffin jumps our way.

"What is it?" I ask as the poor pooch grows in agitation.

The furry cutie takes off, and we follow her all the way behind the café attached to the inn.

Mom and Aunt Ruth stand before us, staring at one another in horror.

And between the two of them, lying facedown with a knife in his back, is an all too familiar man in a pair of turquoise shorts.

Uncle Glenn won't have to worry about making another person angry.

Glenn Pitts is dead.

CHAPTER 3

*H*attie lets out a shrill scream—followed by a shrill scream from Mom and Aunt Ruth. It's a horrible aria I've heard one too many times before, and believe me, I'm more than tempted to join in myself.

Muffin barks and howls, and soon Fish, Cricket, and Sherlock start in on a yowling, howling session of their own.

"I have to call Jasper," I pant as I do just that. A crowd gathers around us and more screaming ensues.

"*Bizzy*," Jasper shouts from somewhere in the crowd as he quickly runs up next to me. "Geez." He winches. "All right, everybody back," he shouts. "Seaview Sheriff's Department here. Please step away from the scene." He pulls out his phone and quickly calls the tragedy into the station. "What happened?" He looks my way.

"Hattie and I were just talking—and Muffin, this cute little thing"—I take a moment to give a gentle scratch over her head —"she came up barking and led us right here." I lean her way. "Muffin, what did you see?"

Hattie nods her way. "Bizzy can hear you, too."

Muffin lets out a soft bark. *I heard Glenn yelling, and by the time I got to him, this is how I found him—with these two women standing over him.*

"Thank you," I tell her before shaking my head up at Jasper. "She heard yelling and then she found him this way— with my mother and Aunt Ruth standing over him."

"We didn't do it!" Mom is quick to insist.

Aunt Ruth shakes her head in a panic. "I would never hurt another living being. You have to believe me," she says, clutching at my mother. "*You* have to believe me, Reeann."

"Oh course, I believe you," Mom says. "I was right here with you."

"All right." Jasper covers his mouth a moment. "Why don't you ladies head down the beach a safe distance? I'll speak with you each in a moment. I'm going to sift for clues."

No sooner does he say the words than the sheriff's department shows up in droves.

"Mother," I say in a panic as I lead both her and Aunt Ruth away from the budding crowd.

"What happened?" Hattie beats me to the question as she looks to her own mother. "For the love of all things good, look me in the eye and tell me you did not shove a knife into that man's back."

"Henrietta Holiday," Aunt Ruth snips. "How could you even ask that question?"

I remember Mom telling me once that she thought the names Aunt Ruth gave her children were stuffy—Henrietta, Winifred, Cornelia, and Henry. I always thought they were cute, and the nicknames the girls go by are even cuter. But I knew back then my mother's comment had more to do with her general dislike of her sister than it did her children's names.

Hattie cringes. "Well, I know how you felt about him. I know how you *both* felt about him."

"Everyone knows how we felt about him." Mom tosses her hands in the air just as Georgie and Macy crop up. "We're doomed."

Macy's platinum blonde hair is cut into a bob around her ears, and she has a pert little nose, along with a gleam in her eyes that can cut any man off at the knees. And that skintight red dress she's donned is designed to do the exact same thing.

Macy swats me on the arm. "Why did you have to go and knock off another one right in the middle of a perfectly good family reunion? Speaking of which..." She glances over her shoulder. "Is it socially acceptable to date a first cousin if you haven't seen him since he was eight? Asking for a friend."

"No," I tell her. "And I didn't off anybody." I glance to the suspects in question. "Start talking, girls."

Georgie sucks in a quick breath. "You girls did the deed, didn't you?" She shakes her head at my mother and Aunt Ruth. "You should have come to me first. I've still got a bad batch of that Passion Potion lying around I could have pumped him full of. And I've got access to an ex-con who

DEATH TAKES A HOLIDAY

knows how to work a backhoe. For fifty bucks I could have pinned it on you-know-who." She hitches her thumb my way.

"Gee, thanks," I say.

"Don't you *gee, thanks* me, missy." Georgie gives me the stink eye. "The least you could have done was wrap him in one of my wonky quilts. It's bad enough Preppy here didn't bring a few to sell to the fam."

Mom is right back to scoffing. "It's nearly two hundred degrees. If I tried to sell one to each of my relatives, they'd all think I was trying to kill them. For your information, I donated one to the raffle."

Georgie makes a face. "If poverty were horses, donations would ride."

"What's a wonky quilt?" Hattie tips her ear my way. "And what's this Passion Potion?"

Macy nods. "A badly stitched blanket and lube." She shrugs. "They sell both down at their shop, Two Old Broads. If it sounds like a genius name, it's because it is. I thought of it myself."

"Mom," I say, stepping in front of her. "Tell me exactly what happened."

She closes her eyes a moment. "Well, Brennan finally showed up with a nice stiff drink." She holds herself and shudders. "And, well, that might have given me the courage I needed when I started up an argument with Ruthie."

Aunt Ruth nods. "We got into a bit of a verbal tussle, and then I suggested we find the louse we had the real beef with."

Macy shakes her head. "Isn't it amazing how Aunt Birdie gets a free pass in all this? If anything, I'd think you'd be equally upset with her."

Mom shakes her head. "Not even I can stay angry with

Birdie for too long. Anyway, I had seen Glenn heading in this direction earlier, so I led the way."

Aunt Ruth inverts her lips. "And that's when we found him."

"Did you hear any arguing?" I ask.

Muffin sure did, and I tend to believe her.

Mom and Aunt Ruth exchange a glance.

"Come to think of it," Mom says. "I did hear him shouting something, but by the time we arrived, he was already flat on his face." *Boy, couldn't he find a different venue to meet up with a killer? I'm not entirely opposed to the scenario—but at the inn? This place really must be cursed. Although, I wouldn't call what happened today a curse, per se. More like a necessary evil.*

Hattie's mouth falls open as she looks to me and I shrug.

What can I say? I tell her. *My mother knows how to hold a grudge like nobody's business.*

"Don't you worry, girls." Georgie slings an arm over each of their shoulders. "Bizzy will bring the killer to justice. Now, all we need to settle on is, who do we want to pin the dirty deed on? Any votes for the foul sister—who is suspiciously *not* in our midst?"

She asks the question just as Aunt Birdie heads this way, breathless.

"I just came out of the bathroom, and I heard the news." Her blouse is soaking wet and her arms look dappled with water beads as well.

"Aunt Birdie," Hattie says. "Why are you doused with water?"

Georgie gives a throaty laugh. "It's obvious, Toots. She killed her ex, jumped into the Atlantic to wash away the evidence, and now she's ready to pin the blame on her sisters. I've heard this country song before." She points to Aunt

Birdie. "Not a bad move on your part, sis. You're someone I'd like to hang out with. Got any killer tips you'd like to share with us? We're just dying to hear 'em. Get it?"

"We get it," I say as I close my eyes a moment. "Why don't the three of you wait here? I'm sure Jasper will want to speak with each of you at length."

"And miss out on my banana pudding?" Birdie balks. "Come on, girls. Let's get us some dessert. We can toast to you-know-whose-first-day-in-you-know-where."

Aunt Ruthie snorts. "And we thought it was hot in Cider Cove."

Mom chortles. "He was a pretty decent running back in college. I bet he's honing those skills once again running from the pitchforks."

Hattie's jaw unhinges in disbelief, and so does my own.

"All right, girls," Georgie says, leading them away. "After the banana pudding, we're getting a round of Hot Lava shots from the bar. It's on Bizzy."

The four of them take off, and Hattie shakes her head.

"They are brutal." She shudders as she says it. As she should. They are pretty brutal.

"*Eh.*" Macy shrugs. "It's just their way of grieving." She juts her head my way. "So when do we hit the nightclubs, trolling for suspects? I'm sure our cousins would love to come along."

And no one protested the idea of me dating Henry, with the exception of my prudish sister. I bet there aren't any laws on the book about it.

"I know that look in your eye, Macy Baker," I tell her. "Cool your coital jets. Henry is off-limits. But if you play nice, he might have a few legal eagle friends he can introduce you to."

Hattie nods. "He has a ton of them, and each one is hotter

than the next. And most all of them are single. You should both come up to Brambleberry Bay after this nightmare is over. We're only an hour away. You'll love it there." *I love it there, minus the unemployed part of the deal.*

I bite down on my lip. "Something will come up," I assure her.

"What?" Macy shakes her head. "We don't wait for suspects to come to us, Bizzy Baker *Milder*. We go after them. I promised Winnie and Neelie I'd show them a good time. I had no idea you were going to pull a body out of a hat. They're only here for a couple of days. We need to chop-chop."

Hattie takes a deep breath. "She's probably right, Bizzy. There are a lot of people who came out for the reunion. I think we need to act quickly."

"You're both right." I sigh as I glance out at the crowd and spot that bald man with the dark beard who was arguing with Uncle Glenn. And he just so happens to be speaking with the man with long flowing hair. "Look at that. I saw both of those men having it out with Uncle Glenn earlier."

Macy groans. "No hotties this go-around, huh?"

I make a face at her. "Excuse her, Hattie. My sister has been known to sink her claws into a suspect or two."

"Or three," Macy volunteers as she frowns over at those two gentlemen. "There goes my streak."

The dogs bound this way and with them is Macy's fluffy white Samoyed, Candy, who happens to have a hot pink rhinestone collar around her neck.

"There's my baby girl." Macy bends over and gives her cutie pie a scratch and a hug. "Don't you dare go look at that body, Candy girl. That's not for your little eyes. You'll have nightmares for a week. Come on, let's go home." She looks up. "It was nice seeing you again, Hattie. I'll be back in the morning. Oh, and I'm going to give you and your sisters a tour of my shop—and my mother's, of course." She rolls her eyes. "Let's hope they keep the Passion Potion to themselves this time."

She takes off with Candy, and both Sherlock and Muffin bark their goodbyes after them.

Muffin jumps in front of Hattie. *What will become of me?*

"Don't worry," I tell her as I give her back a little scratch. "You're welcome to stay with Sherlock, Fish, and me until we straighten everything out."

Cricket mewls, *Sounds like a party. And lucky for me, I'll be around for a couple of days to crash it.*

"We sure will," Hattie says, scooping her up and landing a kiss to her forehead.

Fish hops over and lands in my arms. *I've already told Muffin she could have Sherlock's bed for the night. Feel free to give her his treats as well.*

Sherlock barks. *And I agreed to it.* He licks a line up the side of Muffin's furry face. *Don't worry, girl. We'll take good care of you. Let's go walk along the shore. That always helps me when I'm down.*

They take off and Cricket and Fish bounce right out of our arms and join them.

"At least they get along," I say as Hattie and I make our way back toward the area cordoned off by the sheriff's department. "Too bad no one seemed to get along with Uncle Glenn."

He's finally dead, a somewhat androgynous voice calls out, and both Hattie and I look around at the crowd.

Unless the person whose thoughts I'm listening in on is standing right in front of me, I can't tell if it's coming from a woman or a man.

I can't tell either. Hattie looks my way with a wry smile.

He's gone and I can finally breathe easy, another voice says, this time coming from our left.

Hattie nudges me and nods to our left, where I see my mother, her sisters, and the redhead with the yellow sunglasses who was going at it with both Aunt Birdie and those two men that Uncle Glenn was having it out with.

There he lies, a voice carries from somewhere in the crowd. *I'm not sorry in the least I landed him there. And now I'm going to get away with murder.*

Hattie shakes her head at me. "Not on my watch."

"Not on my watch, either."

CHAPTER 4

*J*t's the very next day, and it's sweltering out even though it's still well before noon. The tourists are plentiful and the Atlantic is majestic.

But I'm not looking at anything majestic right now. I'm standing in the Country Cottage Café looking at what equates to the abomination of desolation taking up her false throne in the holy of holies.

"That's right"—a buxom brunette with full-bodied hair

and a full body leans into the tripod that she's set her phone on—"we're filming live today from the nexus of where Cider Cove's latest tragedy occurred. I'm Camila Ryder and welcome to another episode of *Gossip Gal*. Well, you guessed it. I'm on location. And if I'm on location, that means something big is happening. And that something big would be *murder*. It turns out, the town's infamous snoop, Bizzy Baker, has yet again stumbled upon another body. And I'm going to dissect the case, piece by piece, telling you everything I've gleaned, from eyewitnesses to the whispers of the cove, all the way to what the rumor mill has to say about it. Our first guest is Neelie Holiday. Neelie, I want you to tell me everything that happened yesterday."

"Hey, all!" My cousin Neelie touches her perfectly coiffed blonde hair as she gives a dazzling smile into the camera. "Well, it all started with a family reunion..."

Hattie leans my way. "What in the heck is happening here?"

I make a face at the train wreck in front of us. "That's Camila, my husband's ex- fiancée. She's filming her ridiculous gossip show. Camila was foolish enough to cheat on Jasper with his best friend Leo. I'm not sure if you remember Jasper mentioning Leo yesterday, but Leo is the one who told me all about the transmundane community. He's one of us. And while they were together, he confessed his supernatural skills. So when Camila saw Leo and me seemingly chitchatting without bothering to open our mouths, she sort of deduced that I was telesensual, too. But I never admitted."

"Ugh." Hattie sighs. "That's exactly why I've never told any of my exes. An ex can turn into a *hex* faster than you think."

We share a quiet laugh, and I glance around at the café in the event any of the guests look frightened out of their minds by what's being said. The café is filled with cozy little bistro tables. There's a covered sunroom that leads to the outdoor patio, and from every inch of this place, you can look out and see the sandy shores of the cove.

"I'm sorry Neelie is participating in this madness." Hattie flicks a finger to the carnage still playing out as a small crowd gathers to watch. "But she's sort of a fame-monger."

"No need to apologize. And who knows? This might inspire Neelie to start up a YouTube channel of her own."

"Don't even breathe it. She'd turn Brambleberry Bay on its ear more so than she already has."

A loud squawk comes from the counter, and we turn to find Georgie and Aunt Birdie laughing it up with a giant vat of banana pudding between them.

I shake my head. "Why do I get the feeling this is a potentially explosive situation waiting to happen?"

We head that way, and Hattie takes a seat at the counter. "Banana pudding, please." She sheds a quick grin at Aunt Birdie.

"You betcha," Aunt Birdie says as she looks my way. "I just talked to your cook, and she said the woman who runs this place is out of town. You're running low on desserts, Bizzy. Why don't you let me step in?"

A laugh bubbles from me. "Aren't you on vacation?"

"Being in the kitchen is the only vacation I want. Besides, I'll make up a bunch of my banana pudding. It's quick and easy—and your guests are going to love it."

"Fine by me," I tell her. "Emmie, the woman who heads up the kitchen, is due back in a couple of days, so it'll work out perfectly. Emmie also happens to be my best friend."

Georgie holds up the spoon in her hand. "That's right. They've been thick as thieves since they were tiny tots. They look alike, they walk alike, they talk alike. They even have the same name." She grunts over at Hattie, "Talk about unoriginal."

"It's all true," I say. "We were both christened Elizabeth by our mothers. But to avoid confusion, we've only ever gone by our nicknames."

Hattie looks over. "Is she the one you mentioned was on her honeymoon?"

I nod. "Yup. To Leo Granger." *The telesensual.* "They actually got married at the end of June, but their original honeymoon was laden with one nightmare after the other, so they've been taking long weekends whenever they can. I think this is their third. Come to think of it, Jasper and I should take a page out of their book." Just for the heck of it, of course.

Aunt Birdie's expression sours. "Marriage is overrated if you ask me."

"You tell 'em, Toots," Georgie says, scooping out some more banana pudding from the large footed bowl in front of her. "All that any of my husbands ever wanted was a beer in one hand, the remote in the other hand, and dinner in their mouths."

"They're unreasonable." Aunt Birdie rolls her eyes, and both Hattie and I share a laugh on their behalf because there's not much unreasonable about it.

"Worse yet"—Georgie spikes her spoon into her bowl—"they had the beer, the remote, and the dinner at their *girlfriend's* houses. And not one of them thought to bring me a doggie bag."

Aunt Birdie groans. "I'd laugh if it were funny."

I glance to Hattie. *We should grill Aunt Birdie while we have her cornered. If she didn't do the deed, I'm sure she can point us in the killer's direction.*

Hattie gives a covert nod my way. *Let's shake her down like nobody's business. She's a tough nut. She can take it.*

I lean in to do just that as the back door to the café opens and in runs a menagerie of furry creatures.

Sherlock runs up with Muffin, and they both give a soft woof over to Georgie.

Keep looking cute and innocent, kid, Sherlock tells Muffin. *Georgie can't resist our big puppy dog eyes. She tells me that every time I come around. Just you wait and see, it's about to rain bacon.*

Muffin whines. *I sure hope so. No offense, but Bizzy feeds you dog food. Glenn always gave me his leftovers. He said if it was good enough for him, it was good enough for me.*

"All right, you little beggars, have at it." Georgie stands and empties her pockets of all the salted meat they can hold—and judging by the haul, they can hold an entire pig.

Mom and Aunt Ruth walk in, each holding a smiling feline in their arms, although neither Mom nor Aunt Ruth is smiling themselves.

Fish mewls my way, *Grandma says I'm her comfort creature. She wishes she brought her own cats to the inn, but she's half-afraid they'll get slaughtered.*

Cricket mewls from Aunt Ruth's arms, *That's right. Ruthie thinks they should all pack up and head back to Brambleberry before the Cider Cove curse strikes again.*

Hattie shakes her head at me. *We're not going anywhere, Bizzy. Jasper already made it clear to my mother and my aunt last night that he's glad we're sticking around because he'll need to speak with us.*

I nod her way. *Selfishly, I'm glad about the sticking around part.*

"How was the beach?" I ask the two of them.

Mom grunts, "It was fine until I got hit in the head with a flying Frisbee."

Georgie looks her way. "First, accused of murder, then knocked in the head with a flying object. I wonder what your third strike from the universe will be? Whatever it is, it'll be a doozy. I expect there to be blood."

"Great." My mother flops into the seat next to Georgie. "Why couldn't it be cake?"

"Settle for banana pudding," Aunt Birdie says, sliding a bowl full of the good stuff toward both my mother and Aunt Ruth.

Hattie leans their way. "I'm almost afraid to sound optimistic, but the two of you actually look as if you're getting along."

"She's right," I say. "And the fact one of you didn't end up dead along with Uncle Glenn proves it."

Mom waves her hand at me. "Ruthie actually accused me of doing the deed despite the fact I was with her the whole time."

Aunt Ruth scoffs. "Well, I blinked and you were gone for five minutes, and then you came right back."

"And I told you I wanted more banana pudding, but we were all out."

Aunt Birdie lifts her chin. "That must have been when I ran up to the café to get a refill." Her eyes round out as if she was holding something back, but nary a thought runs through her mind.

Bizzy, Hattie whispers in her mind even though she doesn't have to. *That puts Aunt Birdie at the scene of the crime around that time.*

I nod her way. *All the more reason to grill her.*

Mom and Aunt Ruth exchange a few more barbs, and I'm

about to intervene when I spot my brother, Mackenzie, and Henry stepping into the café.

Hattie and I stride their way.

"Heads-up," I say. "It's raining accusations."

Mackenzie holds her beach ball of a belly. "I wish it was raining amniotic fluid. I can't go another month like this. Who thought it was a good idea to turn a woman into a human incubator the size of a hot air balloon, and then torture her alive for days at a time until she pops? I want names," Mack seethes, and I bite back a laugh. She's wearing a navy tent of a dress, her hair is up in a bun, and somehow she has managed to look every bit as mayoral as she did before my brother helped transform her body into the aforementioned human incubator.

"I'm Hattie, Huxley's cousin," Hattie says to Mack. "We didn't get a chance to meet yesterday before the sheriff's department showed up."

"You mean the Grim Reaper, aka Bizzy Baker." Mackenzie Woods isn't one to mince words.

"*Wilder*," I tell her. "Why does everyone keep forgetting the fact I'm married?" *Conveniently forgetting. Camila does it because it's wishful thinking on her behalf. After all, she still very much has the hots for Jasper. Not that I can blame her. But I can blame her for finagling for herself the position as his secretary at the Seaview Sheriff's Department. I'm still in awe of the level of manipulation that went into securing that feat. And Mackenzie seemingly forgets my legal moniker because she just doesn't care for me all that much.*

I look to Hattie. *Mackenzie is somewhat responsible for this little supernatural quirk of mine, or at least jarring it into me. When we were thirteen, she dunked me in a whiskey barrel full of water at a Halloween party and held me down, nearly drowning me. And since then, I've been terrified of bodies of water, confined spaces, and leery of Mackenzie in general. I managed to stay friends with her up until she stole all of my high school boyfriends, then it was sayonara.*

Hattie chuckles. *I guess her attempted homicide wasn't enough to scare you away. You waited until she murdered your love life.*

That's an accurate assessment, I tell her.

"Hey, Bizzy." Henry pulls me into a quick embrace. He looks a lot like Huxley—dark hair, blue eyes, and same beefy build. They're both in shorts and T-shirts today, eschewing their typical uniform of a suit. "We didn't get a chance to connect too much yesterday. Hux and Mackenzie just gave me the tour of the inn. Over seventy rooms, over three dozen cottages that you lease out, and live in, not to mention the pet daycare facility off the back. You've got a gold mine here."

"Thank you." I laugh. "I used to work here for years before I inherited it from—"

"The man she murdered," Mackenzie finishes for me. "Speaking of the inn, the end-of-summer celebration is set for Saturday right here at the cove. I'm calling it Summer by the Sea. Think fireworks, bonfires, grilled burgers, and whatever dessert you're willing to whip up." Something at the counter snags her attention. "Is there more of that delicious banana pudding we had yesterday? Last night I dreamed I was swimming in a pool of that stuff. Come to Mama." She takes off just as Camila Ryder speeds over.

"Just finished up my show." Camila's eyes are round as silver dollars as she steps in close to Henry. "Camila Ryder, talk show host extraordinaire. Please tell me you're single and that you've just moved to Cider Cove—or Seaview. That's where you can find me and my bedroom, good-lookin'."

Henry gives a nervous laugh, as he should. "Yes to being single, no to living in the area. But I'm not too far. I'm in Brambleberry Bay."

"Brambleberry?" Camila latches onto his arm. "Why, I was just contemplating a move there myself."

"One could only hope," I mutter, and she shoots me a look.

Mom and her sisters head this way, along with Georgie.

"Well, it's settled," Mom says, lackluster. "Birdie has scheduled us to our eyeballs for the day." *Some things never change. She always did have to be in control of how we spent every minute of every day.*

"Where are you off to?" I ask.

Aunt Birdie's lips twist with a hint of mischief. "It's where we're *all* off to. White water rafting up at Birchwood River. It's just thirty minutes from here, and I've already booked us two rafts. Let's get cracking, kids. The day isn't getting any younger. This is going to be a bonding family experience."

"White water rafting?" Hattie looks hesitant. "The last time I tried that, I almost got killed."

"That's because it's *dangerous*," Aunt Ruth cries. *Figures. First, Birdie kills Glenn, and now she wants to off the rest of us.*

Both Hattie and I exchange a nervous laugh.

I'd hate to say it, but Aunt Ruth just might be right.

Here's hoping Aunt Birdie isn't the killer.

Hattie nods. *And here's hoping we don't have a killer good time.*

CHAPTER 5

The Birchwood River is about to offer me two things that I'm deathly afraid of: a body of water that holds the keys to my certain doom and a confined space on the raft I'm boarding that's making me shiver like a dog at the vet.

"Breathe," Hattie whispers. "I promise you'll survive."

"If I don't, I'll be back to haunt you."

Hattie laughs. "I'd welcome the company, so it's not much of a threat."

I texted Jasper and let him know I was about to remove my sanity at the river's edge and partake in my worst nightmare all in the name of the investigation. He texted back and suggested I waited until after the rafting to try to shake down my aunt, but Hattie pointed out that people who are in fear of dying can say the darnedest things—like a confession.

So here I am, stepping into a giant yellow inner tube that looks as if it's just waiting to capsize on us. Aunt Birdie, in an effort to save a dollar, asked if the nine of us could squeeze into an eight-person raft, and the woman at the rental counter said it was up to us.

I begged to be split into two groups. I even offered to pay for the rental of the second raft, but my voice fell on deaf ears. Everyone was already being fitted for a life vest—one I'm positive we'll need.

"We should have opted for the helmets," I say as Huxley helps me into the yellow balloon that might just be responsible for my undoing. But no one says a word. Again, deaf ears.

It's Hux, Henry, my two aunts, my mother, Georgie, Hattie, and me. As soon as Mom called and presented the idea to Macy, my sister laughed so loud you could hear her from the other end of the phone as if she were in the room. Wisely, Neelie and Winnie decided to take the animals for a stroll along Main Street. I should have done the same, but my thirst for justice overrode my need to survive. I really need to rethink this amateur sleuthing thing.

Jasper was right. One of these days I'm going to find myself in over my head with my investigative shenanigans, and I have a feeling that deadly day is upon us.

"We won't need helmets." Henry chuckles at the idea of protecting our gray matter. "Everyone in, and I'll give a few instructions. First and foremost, there's no way back to this part of the river once we take off. The river guides will pick us up at the bottom of our route once we arrive. There's no trail that leads back in this direction either. So if we lose our raft and end up on dry land, we shouldn't separate. It's too dangerous out there. There's too much land and we could easily get turned around."

"Wonderful," I mutter. *Losing our raft and getting lost in the wilderness hadn't even been on my list of things to be paranoid about. But don't worry, Hattie. I've promptly added them.*

The Birchwood River winds its way across a hilly part of the town it's named after. White water rafting is something I suggest to my guests when they ask for adventurous touristy things to do. And yet I've never once taken my own advice and headed this way. For one—water, there's lots of the terrifying wet stuff. And two—the confined space on this balloon could make a coffin feel like a palace. And something tells me not only will I be over my head when I fall to the bottom of this deadly waterway, but I'll be fitted for my own palace soon thereafter.

Since Henry is a pro at this, he's volunteered to be the leader of our raft.

All nine of us squeeze aboard and sink to the bottom of the boat as we struggle to take a seat while a few of the employees of the rental place struggle to hold our raft close to shore.

"Okay." Henry grins as if he were secretly waiting to do just this. "Everyone has to sit on the rim of the raft. That's where we need to be positioned to get our paddles into the water."

"*What?*" I squawk. "We can't sit on the edge of this thing. We'll flip right off."

He's right back to chuckling again as the rest of those around me quickly comply.

"You won't flip right off," Henry says. "That fun won't come until later."

"Not funny," my mother scolds him as she scoots to the edge of the lip of the raft. "Hey? I feel pretty stable."

"You are stable," he assures. "Come on, Bizzy." He helps me sit on the edge, and I can feel an odd case of vertigo coming on as I look down at the water. Although, ironically, the water is just about to my thighs at this point. I knew this was a bad idea. I just didn't realize exactly how bad.

"Don't worry, Bizzy" Hattie links her arm with mine. "If you go down, I'm going down with you."

"That won't work," Camila grunts. "We need you both to paddle."

I frown over at her. *Says the woman in the itsy-bitsy yellow polka dot bikini who made sure to secure her life vest in such a way to showcase what her mama gave her. The good news is, if our life vest drifts away, we can always grab onto Camila and use her body as a floatation device.*

Hattie laughs. *Good one, Bizzy. But you might have to fight Henry for her. He looks pretty smitten.*

I make a face. *Better him than Jasper.*

Aunt Birdie wiggles until she's standing. "I'm not sitting between my sisters. They've been trying to kill each other for years. I'd hate to be a casualty of friendly fire."

"Come here, Birdie Boo," Georgie says as she pats the spot between her and me. Georgie is wearing a bright green kaftan today. If she has her bathing suit on underneath it, she hasn't exposed us to it yet. I'm secretly hoping the

41

kaftan can be used as a parachute in the event of an emergency.

Hattie is right back to giggling. *You're a riot, Bizzy.*

I bet you'd be pretty funny, too, if you thought your life was about to come to a watery end.

She wrinkles her nose. *Sorry.*

Birdie lands next to me and pats my knee. "Didn't I say this would be fun?"

"You said it would be bonding," I remind her. "Fun wasn't promised to anyone."

Georgie rolls her eyes. "You'll have to excuse Bizzy. She's been allergic to fun ever since I've known her."

Hux nods. "She's been allergic to fun ever since I've known her, too."

Mom honks out a laugh. "Maybe she's missing the fun gene?"

Georgie lifts a finger. "That would mean she didn't get any of her dad's genetics." She nods to my aunts. "Ree here isn't exactly a barrel of laughs herself. The first thing she does every morning when I show up for work is try to fire me."

"That's because you keep trying to offer free vodka to our customers," Mom shoots back.

"Then why don't you come up with a better way to get them to open up their wallets?" Georgie snips, and we all share a little laugh on their behalf.

"You're a hoot and a half, Georgie Porgie." Aunt Birdie slaps Georgie on the knee while laughing her head off.

"Georgie's daughter, Juni, is running the store while they're away," I tell her. "She's the other half of the hoot." It's true. Juni inherited all of the chaos, sans the creativity of her mother, which explains her run of prison stints.

The employees hand us each a paddle, and my entire body starts to quiver.

"All right!" Henry motions to the river guides struggling to keep us tethered to the side of God's green earth. "Unleash the beast!"

The employees not only let go, they give us a bionic push as our raft sails quickly into the middle of the river as if it were possessed.

"*Ooh*," I moan as I struggle to maintain my balance. "This was a mistake,"

"Lean in," Henry calls out from the front where he, Hux, and Camila seem to be paddling for their lives as if they know what they're doing—and apparently they do.

If the river were hungry for a soul today, I vote Camila for the sacrifice. That might sound horrible, but I'm not exactly in a benevolent mood right now.

The craft stabilizes to a nice meandering pace, and soon it feels as if we're floating on glass.

"Isn't this wonderful?" Aunt Birdie calls out. "Just feel that fresh air against your face. Look at the rock walls the river is taking us through. To the right, you can see green pastures, verdant with life. Don't you feel alive? If this isn't living, I don't know what is!" She lets out a howl, and the rest of us howl along with her.

A laugh gets caught in my throat as we continue to zigzag our way through a rock formation that looks as if it were set here just for our viewing pleasure.

"This is pretty incredible," I say as adrenaline courses through me like lava through a volcano. "I really do feel alive."

Aunt Birdie howls once again at the top of her lungs, and Georgie chimes in, as they work hard to harmonize their howls.

They're like two werewolves howling at a full moon, Hattie points out.

I couldn't have said it better myself, I tell her. *Is it bad that I'd prefer an entire pack of rabid werewolves to falling in the water?*

Hattie bubbles with a laugh. *The water is so calm I doubt your hair will even get wet.*

Here's hoping.

Hattie nudges me. *Let's start quizzing Aunt Birdie while she's in a good mood.*

I'm with you.

"Can you believe this?" I ask, shaking my head. "It's as if we've stepped outside the realm of reality out here. No one to see us, hear, or judge us. I feel like I can say just about anything."

Aunt Birdie sighs. "Don't I know it. I think we should all take turns shouting affirmations about our beautiful planet. I'll go first. *You are wonderful!*" she calls out with all she's worth.

"Evergreens are my favorite tree!" Mom shouts, and her voice echoes as we enter into a double-walled canyon.

"I love Jasper!" Camila shouts, and I shake my head at her. "What?" she asks, shooting me a look. "It's my favorite stone."

Aunt Ruth raises her paddle. "I love the summer sun on my back!"

Hux nods. "And I love that fall is almost here. That's when I'm going to welcome another Baker into the world."

We all give a howl of approval at that one.

Georgie sits up. "I love rolling around in a meadow, naked with nothing but a dream in my heart! What happens in the meadow stays in the meadow!"

Sounds cryptic, Hattie points out.

Because it is, I tell her.

Hattie clears her throat. "I love the way our voices are echoing," she shouts, and her sentiment is repeated throughout the canyon as if it were rewarding her effort.

"How about you, Bizzy?" Aunt Birdie thumps me on the knee with the butt of her paddle. "What do you want to tell the planet?"

"I—" My lips part just as a rogue wave hits and about a cup of water lands right in my mouth. *"Gah!"* I shriek, and my screams carry in a panicked echo all the way to the stratosphere.

Everyone on the boat has a good laugh on my behalf, and all I can do is glower at the entire lot of them—sans Hattie, of course.

"Never mind." I cough and sputter. "I've probably got ten different amoebas trying to pry their way into my brain via my nasal cavity. I bet everyone will think it's hysterical once my brain dissolves through my nostrils."

"Don't mind her, Toots," Georgie tells Aunt Birdie. "Bizzy's just trying to get all the attention for herself. It wouldn't surprise me if she plucked out her eyeballs and started throwing them at us just to steal the peace and serenity this place has to offer. Speaking of peace, how are you feeling now that a little deadweight has been eliminated from your life?" *Don't worry, Biz,* Georgie says. *I know what you're up to. I'll pump this little bird fountain of information until the name of the killer spouts from her lips. And if the killer is on this raft, I say what happens in Birchwood stays in Birchwood, if you catch my drift.*

I nod. Although that eyeball plucking thing was a little more than weird. But for the most part, I've come to appreciate Georgie's investigative style. I'm not sure I'd have it in me to turn my family over to the sheriff's department. Jasper might be on his own with this one.

"Deadweight?" Aunt Birdie guffaws at the morbid pun. "That's a good one. If Glenn is anything, he's deadweight."

"I still can't believe someone shoved a knife in his back," I say, hoping to steer the conversation.

"I sure can," Aunt Birdie says, paddling all that much faster. "The man was diabolical. On our wedding day, he had me sign a few papers while I was getting ready for my walk down the aisle. He told me there were just a few last-minute things that concerned the ceremony. Turns out, he was locking me out of the dealership. I told him it was a fruitless move. I'm his wife. Any judge would have sided with me to get half of it." *Although my attorney told me point-blank it wasn't looking too good.* She sighs. *And I won't admit in a boat full of family that we kept separate bank accounts the entire time we were married. He knew my bistro was struggling. He knew I was moments from shutting the doors forever, and yet that SOB wouldn't give me a dime. Well now, I'll get all the dimes in the world, and I'm not too sorry about it. I should have taken him to court the second I found out about his first hussy.*

Hattie gasps. "Aunt Birdie, do you think Uncle Glenn was cheating on you?"

Aunt Birdie averts her eyes. "Please. It was no secret the man didn't know how to keep it in his pants. Ask half the women on this vessel."

I'd rather not.

"Is that why you separated?" I ask. She did just mentally rattle off a few good reasons, though.

"I'm ashamed to say I let a few of his floozies fly under the radar." She lowers her voice a notch so that my mother and Aunt Ruth can't hear us from across the way. "I knew my sisters were just waiting to say I told you so. Ree warned me that I'd lose him how I got him, and she was right." She looks up at me. "Your mother is right about everything. I couldn't stand that about her."

Georgie leans in. "We can't stand that about her either. I say we jab her with a paddle and watch her fall to a watery grave."

I choose to ignore Georgie's homicidal proposal.

"So you finally hit your limit?" I ask Aunt Birdie as we go over a rolling wave and a collective *ooh* circles our raft.

"That's right." Aunt Birdie doesn't hesitate to admit it. "In fact, his latest floozy had the nerve to show up yesterday. Coral Shaw, the redhead you saw me chewing out. She's some fancy schmancy snoot. But in all honesty, they weren't a couple until after Glenn got his own place. I think Coral used to be married herself until recently. We were cordial acquaintances for a while. She's worked at the dealership forever."

"Oh? Is she an accountant?" Hattie asks. *Maybe Coral killed him because she's been embezzling money?*

I like how you think, I tell her.

"No." Aunt Birdie is quick to pop our money-grubbing bubble. "She's a saleswoman. A darn good one, too. It was because of her that I suggested Glenn stop calling them salesmen and switch to *salesperson*. It was so chauvinistic."

Georgie shakes her head. "It's a man's world, and we're just living in it."

"Well, he's not living anymore," Aunt Birdie says. "Someone thought Glenn didn't deserve his next breath." *I'd agree, but it might make me look guiltier than I already do.* "But with your husband on the case, Bizzy, I'm sure the killer won't remain free for too long." *Ha. Ree says the man hasn't solved a case in years. It's Bizzy who does all the heavy lifting. Just like a man, leave it to a woman to do what he can't handle.*

I bite my lip as I look to Hattie and shrug. *He does try.*

"Aunt Birdie?" I shout as we go over the top of a wave and glide right down it. "Who do you think could have done something like this to Uncle Glenn?"

She purses her tiny lips. "I don't know, but I'd suggest your husband start snooping around that dealership. I heard Glenn saying something to Coral yesterday about not letting them get away with murder. I'm pretty sure it had to do with money. Although, at the end of the day, the phrase took on a much broader meaning." *A far more literal one.*

Hattie looks my way. *I guess we know where we're going next. Coral Shaw just might have the answers we seek to clear our mothers' good names.*

I'm about to agree when the raft takes a sharp turn. The rapids grow wild, white as snow, and violent, as we struggle to paddle and stay afloat. We're tossed to the left and right, and soon one wave after another lands on top of us.

I scream bloody murder, and as I tip my head back, the raft lurches, and I fall backward to that certain doom I had predicted.

The icy water swallows me in one ravenous gulp.

Can't breathe.

I'm going to die.

Jasper is going to kill me.

Fish will never forgive me.

Sherlock will hope Jasper's next wife actually knows how to cook bacon.

My voice rubs raw as my screams dare to peter out.

"Bizzy!" Georgie calls out, and I can see her belly flopping into the water after me.

Screams sizzle from my throat as I thrash wildly, trying to get my footing while the river washes both Georgie and me downstream.

Henry runs to the end of the raft and holds out his paddle as Georgie, me, and the raft in question are moving at a breakneck pace down the twisting river. And it's the *breakneck* part that has me rethinking my life choices.

"I've got it," Georgie shouts, latching onto the oar, and without missing a beat, I latch onto her leg.

Mom casually turns this way as if to see what all the commotion is about.

"*Bizzy!*" Mom screams as she leaps in after us just as the water pushes us like a tidal wave.

Soon, Huxley is in the water, and Aunt Ruth, then Aunt Birdie—as my brother does his best to collect us all like loose leaf papers blowing in the wind.

Georgie holds onto the paddle while the rest of us hold onto Huxley's limbs for dear life, and we race our way down that river like a human cannonball.

The raft crashes against the side of an embankment, and the rest of the crew falls off, and one by one we all crawl up onto the shoreline.

Hattie helps me along until I'm lying on a bed of hot grass with my face to the earth as I pant like mad.

"I'll never do that again as long as I live." I hug the ground and take in all the warmth it gives me.

Aunt Birdie and Georgie are back to howling as they link arms and dance in a circle, bragging about how good it feels to be alive.

"Too bad Uncle Glenn can't brag about that," Hattie says.

"The killer won't be bragging for long either," I say. "As

soon as I walk back down to wherever it is we parked, we'll make plans to track down Coral Shaw."

"Bizzy, you can't walk back to the car. It's too far. Henry says it's another couple miles to the pickup at the bottom of the river and there's no trail in this direction. He says we shouldn't separate. It's too dangerous to go off on our own, remember?"

I look up to find Camila trying her best to gnaw off Henry's face and frown at the sight.

What does Henry know? He's fallen under Camila's spell and can't be trusted.

"Good luck getting me back on that raft," I say, sitting up. "If it's too dangerous to go off on our own, I guess I'll need someone to come with me."

And Hattie does just that.

It takes us hours to get back to the rental dock, and by that time the sun is about to set and the search parties were about to be deployed.

So much for tracking down another suspect tonight. I can't see straight, walk straight, or think straight.

Here's hoping tomorrow I can feel my feet.

Whoever the killer is, they can thank the Birchwood River for buying them another day of freedom.

But just like Uncle Glenn's life, that freedom is about to run out.

CHAPTER 6

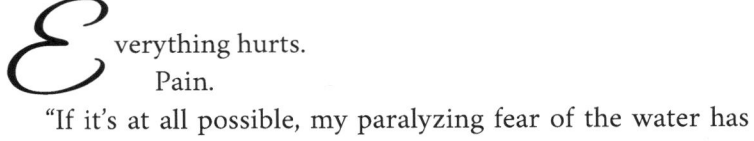

*E*verything hurts.
     Pain.

"If it's at all possible, my paralyzing fear of the water has increased tenfold," I say to Hattie as we walk down Main Street through the treacherous sun, thick humidity, and even thicker summer crowds.

"I'm sorry." Hattie sighs. Her dark hair is pulled back into a ponytail and she's donned a lavender sundress that hugs her figure. "But if it's any consolation, I can promise you, the water isn't out to get you."

"That's what you think."

It's the very next day after our white water horror, and we're headed to Two Old Broads where Mom is about to show off both her store and Macy's shop to my aunts and cousins. My aunts chose to drive because they didn't want anything to do with the heat wave we're going through.

Smart women.

My cousins walked as well, but they left a little earlier than we did since they didn't have any pets to wrangle. And I'm more than glad to have a minute alone with Hattie. Now that we know all about our shared gift, we have a lifelong bond that we're only beginning to nurture.

Fish mewls up at me contentedly and lands a paw to my chest.

Typically, I carry her around in one of those wonky pet carriers that Georgie gave me—coincidentally the same one they sell for infants—but I couldn't fathom putting another layer on my flesh today. The general public is lucky I'm not walking around nude. Apparently, not only do I not do well with water or confined spaces, I'm not so keen on impossibly hot weather.

What did you find out about the killer yesterday? Fish twitches her whiskers at both Hattie and me before looking over at Cricket. *Bizzy passed out as soon as she got home. She even forgot to feed us. Sherlock practically had to bite Jasper's ankle off before he got the hint.*

"It's true," I confess. "I apologized up and down once I woke up and fed them all enough for three days. Thankfully, Jasper did feed them last night, but poor Muffin snubbed the kibble. I tried wet dog food this morning and she looked at me as if I was nuts."

The fluffy little furball turns my way. *That's because you are nuts if you think I'd take a bite out of that. I don't mean to be a picky eater, but when you've been raised on burgers and fries, that wet goop isn't as appealing.*

Sherlock barks and jumps. *I want burgers and fries! Let's change my diet, Bizzy. What do you say? Think of all the time you'll save buying dog food. And remember that day you almost threw out your back trying to carry a bag of kibble from the car to the cottage? Jasper said that job wasn't for you.*

Fish yowls, *That's because the bag weighed as much as a body.*

Cricket mewls over at Fish, *Why does dog food come in obnoxiously large bags, anyway? Hattie and I have seen them at the store, and they look horrific.*

Fish mewls back, *Because dogs are obnoxious.*

Cricket yowls, *That should be a hint to people, of things to come with those hairy scary beasts. No offense, Sherlock and Muffin, but if the bag fits.*

Hattie and I share a laugh.

"Play nice," I tell Fish.

"Seriously, though," Hattie says as we come upon my mother and Georgie's shared business venture. "Those bags are one of the reasons I may never get a dog. I wouldn't be able to lift the food they'd need just to survive."

Muffin turns back our way. *There's an easy solution. Don't feed your pooch dog food.* She looks to Sherlock. *We should start a campaign.*

A revolution! Sherlock barks with glee.

See that? Fish meows. *One simple walk down Main Street*

with two canines and a revolution is born—an unnecessary one for that matter.

Cricket snorts. *And one simple walk down Main Street with two felines and both of our girls are calmer for the effort.* She looks up at Hattie. *Maybe you can rent me out by the hour? I could be one of those fancy comfort creatures. That way we won't lose our rental and have to move in with your mother.*

"Oh no." I look to Hattie. "I'm so sorry. I didn't think it was that bad. Of course, it's that bad. I mean, you're out of work. I can always find you something to do at the inn if you like. And it wouldn't have to be a commute. You could live at the inn while you're here. It'll be fun."

Hattie squints to the sky as if considering it. "That's a very generous offer, and believe me, it's tempting, but I really need to build a life in Brambleberry. Winnie has her craft shop, and Neelie has her constant schemes and dreams. Thank goodness she's not doing time—the entire family worries about her. And Henry is a top attorney in the area—very much in demand with both his clients and women."

"Is your dad still running his fishing boats?" I remember Uncle Henry being such a kind man—and completely devoted to Aunt Ruth. One year he dressed as Santa and gave out gifts to each of the kids at the Christmas party that my grandmother threw—one of the rare moments my mother was in the same room with her sisters. I got a teddy bear and I slept with him in my arms straight through high school. Not that I would breathe a word of that to anyone.

Hattie chuckles. "I won't breathe a word of it either. And by the way, I remember that party. I got the same bear, and I may or may not have done the very same thing. I knew I liked you." She bumps me with her elbow. "And yes, my dad's still got his boats. Three lobster boats, to be exact. He's doing well, and my mother is in every social club known to man."

"You're lucky to have such a great family. I can see why you wouldn't want to leave Brambleberry."

"Thanks. I think so, too. How's your dad?"

"He's fine. He's still feeding his matrimonial addiction. In fact, it's colliding with his addiction to cruises. He's married to my mother-in-law now. And yes, it's as weird as it sounds."

We come upon Two Old Broads with its red double door entry and head inside where we're instantly refreshed with the cool air-conditioning.

"Oh, I can breathe," Hattie says as she takes a quick look around at the bay window, the rustic wood floors, and the counter in the back. "Wow, this place is adorable!"

Come on, Muffin. Sherlock barks. *I know where Georgie keeps the treats.*

They wouldn't happen to be donuts, would they? Muffin asks.

Nope. They're better. They're doggie biscuits!

Here we go again, Muffin says as she waddles as fast as she can to keep up with Sherlock.

Cricket sits up in Hattie's arms. *Look at all the colors.*

"She's not wrong," I say to Hattie. "Two Old Broads specializes in wonky quilts, which not only come in every color, but they come in every size. They've got a pet line, a bridal line, a children's line, and are constantly scheming to turn their wonky quilts into new and exciting products. A couple of months ago they started selling some magic oil Georgie concocted that could be used for a variety of things from achy muscles to"— I make a face—"something connected to a very coital matter. Let's just say that ended badly. Stinging nettle was involved, as well as dozens of pending lawsuits that

Hux had to deal with. But Mom and Georgie are still on the hunt for their next big product." I point to the right where a sign reads *Ree's Priceless Picks*. "This is my mom's official half of the store," I say, nodding to the racks of clothing that could make every preppy on the planet drool, neatly folded quilts of her choosing, candles, and knickknacks.

"A place for everything and everything in its place," Hattie says.

"And that"—I look to the left side of the store—"is Georgie's half." Quilts and a few of her mosaic art pieces sit jumbled over a couple of tables.

A few barrels are scattered around, filled with beans, and a handful of antique bottles are scattered on top. A sign sitting on the floor, in the middle of the melee, reads *Georgie's Junk. Get it while it's hot!* And each letter is comprised of pieces of broken glass. "Georgie is actually an artist who specializes in mosaics. She made the mosaic mural that runs along half of Main Street."

"You bet your sore bottom, I did," Georgie says as she runs this way with her pink and white kaftan trailing after her. "Give me these cutie pies," she says, scooping both Cricket and Fish out of our arms, and the cats give a collective yowl. "Come on, girls. The Pahrump sisters are just getting ready to dish the dirt and spill all the family secrets. I bet ten bucks there's a killer in the mix."

We scuttle along with her to the counter where Mom and her sisters are congregating along with Macy, Winnie, and Neelie.

I wave to Juni as she works the register while a smattering of customers make their purchases.

Juni is pretty much a carbon copy of Georgie minus

twenty years. She prefers to dress as if she belongs in a biker gang and loves long walks on the wild side.

"And here's the star of the show." Juni chortles as she looks my way. "I heard all about how you went skin surfing down the Birchwood River."

"That's right," Mom says. "And she took the rest of us along with her."

Georgie shakes her head at me. "Boy, you're bad luck, kiddo." She looks to my aunts and cousins. "I wouldn't follow this one into a potentially hazardous situation."

"Or a potential safe situation," Macy adds, and our little circle lights up with laughter.

Mom shakes her head. "At least there wasn't a body at the end of that fiasco. I swear, killers choose a venue they know Bizzy will be at—much to their detriment."

Aunt Birdie waves it off. "Had I known Bizzy was that good at tracking down a killer, I would have plunged a knife into Glenn somewhere else."

Muffin barks and nobody laughs.

"Oh, come on." Aunt Birdie rolls her eyes. "You know I didn't do it." *So much for making everyone laugh. I've only managed to make myself look guiltier than I already am.*

Than she already is?

Hattie and I exchange a look.

"Stop it, girls," she says to the two of us. "No, I didn't kill him. And if I did, I would have hired someone to do the deed. The last thing I'd want is blood on my hands. Banana pudding, anyone?"

We all give a resounding yes and Mom helps Aunt Birdie pass out plastic cups brimming with the yummy confection.

"So where were we?" Aunt Ruth scrunches her shoulders

near her ears. She has her hair in a bun and looks impeccably put together in a floral shift dress and wedges.

Mom nods to Hattie and me. "I was just about to tell them about some of the history my grandmother passed down to me. First of all, my grandfather was a gold prospector and had a few claims that produced a nice living for him and my grandmother."

"That's right." Aunt Birdie fluffs out her blonde mane with her fingers. "And did you know we had a direct relative who was tried and hanged as a witch way back when?"

"*No.*" Winnie gasps. "Oh, that's awful." *But don't think I won't use this to boost my Halloween sales at the store. I'm going to find out her name and turn her into a star. Poor thing.*

Hattie shrugs. *Her heart is in the right place, but she does like to earn a profit.*

"That's right," Aunt Ruth says. "They accused her of reading people's minds. Can you imagine? I guess she had a knack for knowing what someone was thinking and called out the mayor for having an affair, in addition to lewd thoughts about half the women in that town."

She read minds? I shoot Hattie a look. *I see now our genetic quirk runs deep.*

She nods. *Good thing we were born centuries later.*

Aunt Birdie lifts her spoon. "What about Great Aunt Edna?"

The three Pahrump sisters break out into a laugh.

Mom looks our way. "She was a psychic who worked with the circus. She made money hand over fist. The people just loved her."

"No, no." Aunt Ruth shakes her head. "She wasn't a psychic. I think she, too, claimed she could read minds."

Aunt Birdie shakes her head. "It wasn't either of those. She worked one of those let me guess your weight, height, the year you were born types of things. But she also guessed occupations, how many children people had and their names. She was pretty phenomenal."

Another mind reader, I bet, I say to Hattie.

"How's the circus looking to you, Hattie? That might land you a nice, fat paycheck," Neelie teases with her red lipstick grin. Neelie could easily be a cover model, with her glossy blonde hair and twig-like limbs. But you can definitely see a hint of mischief in her eyes.

"That's funny." Winnie nods with a laugh, and that dark bun sitting on top of her head wobbles. "Or maybe you could open a psychic booth on the beach up in Brambleberry? Nobody has to know you're a fake."

"You're hysterical." Hattie averts her eyes. "But sadly onto something considering my prospects are slim."

"Ooh, make it a kissing booth." Macy wiggles her shoulders. "I've heard rumors of those Brambleberry boys. I'd definitely come up and visit. Seriously, though, you should consider opening up a soap and candle shop. I make a killing with the markup. The key is to trick the customers into believing they're getting a deal. I mark up my inventory so much I make the customers believe that if they buy two they get one free, when in reality they're paying a premium for all three products."

A group of women nearby gasp, and Macy shakes her head at them.

"They only do that at Two Old Broads. Run across the street to Lather and Light and get a *real* discount. Use the code words *Two Old Broads Stink* to get an additional fifteen percent off."

An entire herd of women trot out the door.

"Gee, thanks," Mom says, digging her fists into her hips.

Georgie gives Macy the stink eye. "Now it's time to plot my retribution. Remember, missy, you've forced my hand. Don't come crying to me when nary a customer blinks in your direction. The customer wars are on."

"You drew first blood, Macy," Mom says with an aggressive nod.

Aunt Ruth laughs. "Ree, it's nice to see you're as forgiving today as you were way back when."

Mom's expression turns on a dime. "I guess I have you to thank for that. It's hard to forgive when someone you trust goes behind your back and gets engaged to the man you thought you'd have a family with."

Macy shudders as she looks my way. "We could have been the Pitts sisters."

"And it would have been the pits," Aunt Birdie teases. "Oh, come on. He's dead. You should both feel better. Ree, you know Ruthie is about as gullible as they come. He probably fed her a mountain of lies."

Aunt Ruthie scoffs. "I am not gullible." Her lips twitch. "I just believed him when he said that Ree wanted the two of us to be together."

"Why in the world would you believe something so asinine?" Mom's voice edges toward the sound barrier.

"Don't answer that," Aunt Birdie says. "I know something that can make us all feel better—especially me. The Pitts Stop sits within a conglomerate of dealerships, and they happen to be having their annual summer days festival. It's a complete carnival with a couple of rides, some games, a few of those jump houses, and food geared to spike our cholesterol levels. We should head over and have some fun while checking out my future dealership. Who's in?"

Winnie claps. "I'm in. I just love a good carnival. And there always seems to be a craft booth or two. I'll consider it research."

Neelie shrugs over at Macy. "We could scope out the men, and if we don't like the clowns we see, we can move on to the salesmen. And if we don't like what we see there, there's always funnel cake."

Macy waggles her brows. "Sounds like a win-win situation to me."

"You had me at funnel cake," Georgie says.

"I'll invite Henry," Aunt Ruth says as she whips out her phone.

I nod to Hattie. "And we can tour the dealership."

She smiles my way. *Here's hoping we can get Coral Shaw herself to give us that tour.*

CHAPTER 7

True to Aunt Birdie's word, there is a full-blown carnival taking place at the Edison Auto Mart, complete with a Ferris wheel, a whirly-twirly ride that looks as if it turns you into a spinning human centrifuge before it demands you puke your guts up, and a few kiddie rides and jumpers that have toddlers lined up by the droves.

Then there's the food. Globs of pink and blue cotton

candy, funnel cakes, corndogs, street tacos, and churros circulate through the crowd.

"I hardly know where to start first," Georgie says as she holds Sherlock on a leash.

I've got Muffin on a leash and Macy brought Candy. Both Fish and Cricket are in a wonky quilt carrier strapped to my chest, the very carrier I was glad to eschew on such a hot day. But seeing that we might need our hands free, Hattie and I decided we'd trade off strapping the kitty-laden heat bomb to our bodies.

What is that thing? Cricket asks while looking up at one of the zippy, flippy rides they have going. *And please tell me you won't be going on it.*

"No way," Hattie says. "I'm not big on turning my stomach upside down. I'm more of a put-things-in-my-stomach kind of a girl. How about a corndog before we head to the dealership?"

Georgie pats her belly. "I like your line of thinking." She nudges my mother who is deep in conversation with my aunts. "How about we hop in a food line and bust our bellies with enough carnival fare to fill a supermarket with?"

They all enthusiastically agree and we settle into the line at the nearest corndog stand. Macy and Neelie have already started their manhunt, in the literal sense. Macy brought Candy because men seem to magnetize to cute critters just as much as women do. And Winnie is off admiring hand-painted signs with clever sayings like *no trespassing—hiding bodies is exhausting, pets welcomed—people tolerated,* and *I miss my ex-husband, but my aim is getting better.*

Mom and Aunt Birdie laughed extra-long at that last one.

We get our corndogs and Georgie gets two, one for each hand.

The corn batter is thick and perfectly golden brown. It tastes as if I were eating the best deep-fried cornbread known to man.

"This is gourmet," I insist as I indulge in another bite.

"These are so good." Aunt Birdie groans through each bite of her own. "I wish I were as smart as you, Georgie. I could have easily eaten two."

Muffin barks. *So could I. Who knew that if anything happened to Glenn I'd be forced to starve to death? And at the hands of such nice people, too.*

"All right, cute stuff." Georgie plucks the stick out of one of her corndogs—then pretends to lose her grip as it sails to the floor.

Both Muffin and Sherlock dive for it and Muffin growls at Sherlock as if a bar brawl were about to break out. *You haven't missed a meal yet, Sherlock. And the only thing I'm running off of is the bacon that rains from Georgie's pockets.*

Okay, fine. Sherlock sulks before flashing those puppy dog eyes up at Georgie once again and her second corndog goes flying sans the stick as well.

Aunt Birdie laughs. "How about we do a quick tour of the dealership, and then I'll buy you another set of corndogs, Georgie?"

"Sounds good to me," Georgie says. "I hear they have boxes of donuts lined up in those places."

"They typically do," Aunt Birdie says. "But Glenn was way too cheap to do that. His motto was *the employees get nothing—and neither does my ex.*"

We all have a chuckle on Uncle Glenn's frugal behalf.

Fish mewls up at me, *Come to think of it, Bizzy, you don't serve donuts to your staff either.*

Sherlock gives a soft woof. *Jasper loves donuts. He once told me that was his favorite part about working at the station.*

I make a face as I look to Hattie. "Camila Ryder of *Gossip Gal* fame is the provider of the donut boxes."

Hattie shakes her head. "That girl has moves."

"You bet she does." Mom points over to the Ferris wheel. "Camila's right there and she looks as if she's making out with someone."

"That had better not be Jasper," I tease, but end up having a mild heart attack when I see her victim's dark hair and the fact he's wearing the same kind of suit Jasper dons for work.

"It's Henry." Aunt Ruth's mouth falls open. "Well, how do you like that? We come to Cider Cove and Henry makes a love connection."

Hattie laughs. "I don't think love has anything to do with any of the connections Henry makes with women. It's more of a connection of convenience."

Aunt Birdie squints at the scene. "Glenn and I necked on a Ferris wheel when we first met."

"Sounds about right," Aunt Ruth smarts. "You stole him from me just in time for the summer fair."

Mom shakes her head at Aunt Ruth. "And you stole him from me at the Christmas parade. Not only did you ruin my relationship, but you ruined my holidays."

"Yeah, yeah," Georgie says, slinging an arm over my mother's shoulder. "But I bet the next year that followed was pretty spectacular."

Mom tips her head to the side. "You know what? It was. I met Nathan, the next not-so-great love of my life, and that led to having three pretty great kids."

"See there?" Aunt Ruth links arms with my mother. "I was practically doing you a favor."

"You didn't do *me* any favors," Aunt Birdie says as we move through the heat, all the way to the Pitts Stop Dealership. "But then again, after a little legal finagling, this place will be all mine. I guess you did me a favor after all, Ruthie." *And I just might have the money to save my bistro. I guess Glenn wasn't kidding when he said I could have the money over his dead body.*

Hattie and I bite down on a laugh over that one.

A giant spinning sign sits on top of the roof of the palatial dealership that my uncle owned and reads *Need a deal or a steal? Let the Pitts Stop drive you into the future.*

An entire sea of sedans, minivans, and trucks sits outside of the facility along with rows and rows of colorful balloons.

We head in through the glass doors and a blast of frigid air welcomes us.

"This feels like heaven." Hattie sighs.

"Glenn couldn't have been that cheap," Mom says. "Air-conditioning a building of this size, with vaulted ceilings no less, must have cost him a fortune."

"Just great." Aunt Birdie gives the stink eye to the place as if it were Uncle Glenn himself. *And there goes some of my new fortune.*

A friendly chortle erupts to our left, and we look to see the exact woman Hattie and I were hoping to see, Coral Shaw.

She's tall, and her red hair is loose and wavy around her face, cut to her shoulders in a modern bob. She has on a breezy mint green pantsuit, and a pink floral scarf hangs around her neck.

"I wondered when you would show up." She sheds a genuine smile while giving both Sherlock and Muffin a quick pat. "Oh, we've missed our cute little Muffin." She gives a solemn nod to Aunt Birdie. "I'm sorry for your loss."

"And I'm sorry I ever blamed you for anything. You were

the only woman Glenn was with that he didn't technically cheat on me with. My apologies for being terse with you the other day. All of my terse words were meant to hurt him."

Coral waves it off. "Don't even think about it. I've got an ex myself. We've been separated for a year, and we're just now getting to the divorce." *That's because I have to pay for the entire disaster. I should have known I'd be cleaning up his messes right to the bitter end.*

Sounds horrible, Hattie says, and I nod in agreement.

"I'm sorry to hear it," Aunt Birdie says. "I hope you don't mind if I give these gals the grand tour."

"Not at all."

Aunt Ruth clasps her hands together. "I can't wait to see your new office, Birdie."

Mom makes a face. "You might want to disinfect it. We all know what he liked to do behind closed doors."

They break out into warm laughter and Coral giggles along with them.

Coral takes a breath. *I guess they know him well enough to realize I wasn't the only one he was doing that with back there. Come to think of it, I never once saw Birdie head back there with him. Glenn really was a louse.*

"Go right ahead," Coral tells her. "If you need anything at all, especially a great deal on a car, I'm your girl." She winks as Aunt Birdie speeds off with Aunt Ruth and my mother. But Georgie, Hattie, and I stay behind to have at our mark.

"So the rumors are true." Georgie sniffs around with a look of disappointment on her face. "Glenn hated paying for donuts."

"You bet." Coral has another laugh on Glenn's behalf—not an uncommon phenomenon. "But he was a pretty big fan of Julian's by the Sea. It's a bar and grill out on Whaler's Wharf.

He had a buffet spread for the employees every day in the lounge."

"Wow," I marvel. "Talk about generous. That place isn't only the happening party scene, but they have a menu with prices that are out of this world."

"And a renowned reputation," Hattie says. "Everyone knows about Julian's back home because he's opening a location in Brambleberry."

Coral nods. "That's right. I think Julian mentioned it. Julian Richards himself used to drive the food over." She cringes a moment.

Georgie moans. "The food was bad, wasn't it, Toots? You can tell us, you're among friends. Besides"—she hitches her thumb at me—"Bizzy is too cheap to take me out to some snazzy seafood place. She said if I behaved, she might throw a corndog at me later."

A laugh strums from me. "I said no such thing."

Georgie groans. "See that, Red? I act up and it's no corndog for me."

Hattie looks to Coral. "So if the food wasn't bad, what had you cringing at the mention of the man? Should my small town be wary of him?"

Wary is an understatement. She forces a smile. *It's not like I'm going to rat Julian out to these women. Certainly one of them is in the market for a new car. I'd hate to put them in a bad mood. It's bad enough they might be grieving.*

Rat Julian out? I look to Hattie.

Fish lands a paw on Cricket. *Oh, this must be good.*

Cricket nods. *I bet it's juicy. Maybe this woman is the killer?* A yowl comes from her.

"You poor, sweet thing." Coral digs Cricket out of my carrier. "Oh, how I miss having a cat, yes, I do," She rubs her cheek to Cricket's forehead. *I'd have ten cats if I knew I wouldn't be battling them for cat food. Glenn was lying when he said these cars practically sold themselves. Thankfully, he's gone, and I can continue to suck the funds out of this place.*

Both Hattie and I gasp at the very same time.

She's stealing, I say.

Hattie nods. *And I bet he caught her, so she killed him before he could go to the police.*

Help, Cricket yowls again. *A killer has got me in her clutches! I'm going to be next! She's going to find the nearest knife, and I'll lose all nine lives at once from fright!*

Muffin gives a soft bark. *Coral is pretty nice. But I did hear her and Glenn arguing a lot lately.*

My lips part as I look to Hattie. *That cinches it,* I tell her. *She's a thief and most likely the killer.*

Georgie narrows her gaze at the woman. "So tell me, Toots. I've been thinking about getting into the automobile game. I'd like to know what's ahead. What kind of a lifestyle are we talking? Beer or champagne?"

Coral gives a throaty laugh. "Oh, honey, if I'm not having champagne, life isn't worth living. My ex-husband spoiled me rotten so I can't be blamed. He bought us a nice house out on the bluff in Whaler's Cove, Italian clothes, cars, a collection of sapphires in every hue they come in, and not one but *two* Arabian horses."

"Woo-wee!" Georgie slaps her hands together. "Sounds like I need to get into *his* line of work. What does he do, and more importantly, is he still single?"

Coral bucks with laughter as she slaps her thigh. "He's into investment banking. And believe me, you wouldn't want to get tangled up with him. Let's just say he's under the watchful eye of the authorities. The man was nothing but trouble and heartache. But I'm too proud of a woman to suckle off that scammer. I'm making pretty good financial inroads myself." She winks over at her.

"You must be a whiz at making cars fly off the lot," I say.

Hattie glances my way. *She'd have to be just to maintain that lifestyle. I've boarded horses. Nothing about those beautiful beasts comes cheaply.*

"Oh, I am." Coral straightens. "I outsell these boys every night of the week." She leans in as if she was about to fill us in on something juicy. "I've made top salesperson for the past six months."

"Congratulations," Hattie says in awe. *We'd better be careful, Bizzy, or all three of us might be leaving with a new set of wheels.*

Georgie juts her head in Coral's direction. "So what's Julian's dirty secret? Maybe I can blackmail him with it and score a free lobster dinner out of the deal."

Coral laughs and gives Cricket a strangulating embrace. "Actually, Julian did have some sort of a secret. Or at least he had something between him and Glenn that he didn't want anyone else to know about. They went into Glenn's office the past few times Julian came by, and I heard them yelling at the top of their lungs, but no matter how hard I tried to listen in I couldn't make head or cute furry little cat tails out of it." She picks up Cricket's tail and kisses the tip.

"Arguing with Julian?" I inch back. *The plot thickens.*

Indeed, Hattie says. "Has Julian said anything about Glenn's passing?"

"No, actually," Coral's shoulders bounce, "he hasn't come by since Glenn passed away. The staff is really bummed about it, too. A few of us are brown bagging it and the rest have gone off-site for lunch. You don't know how much money you save by getting a free hot meal every day." *Boy, do I ever miss it.* "And a lobster lunch to boot."

"Uncle Glenn was pitching for lobster?" I marvel.

"Yes," Coral says. "Julian brought quite a spread."

Hattie leans in. "How long did this go on for?"

"Oh, it's been happening now for about six months. At first, there were just a few sandwiches, but this last month Julian started to roll out the red carpet."

"Was this happening at about the same time he was having these arguments with Glenn?" I ask.

Coral inches back. "Come to think of it, yes." *Wow, I never knew how perfectly Julian would factor into this.* Her eyes open wide. "I just thought of something." She snaps her fingers. "I saw Julian at that family picnic where Glenn was killed."

"You did?" I tip my ear her way. "I'm actually the owner of the inn where the event was held. Can I ask what Julian looks like?" I'm sure I could look him up on the internet, but if Coral can help, all the better.

"Bald, dark thick beard." She glances to the ceiling. "And he's a great dresser. One of those guys who loves to wear a bowtie everywhere he goes."

Georgie nods. "In other words—he's a hottie."

Coral laughs. "I don't know if I'd go that far."

The visual of him comes in crisp, especially when I remember what he was doing.

"I saw him there that day, too," I say as I look to Hattie. "He was arguing with Uncle Glenn."

She nods. "I remember thinking they were about to come to blows."

"Well, there you go." Coral slaps her palms together. *Thank goodness they both remember Julian. And a knife? That would be the exact murder weapon someone like Julian would use.*

I nod in agreement even though she didn't say those words out loud.

"And I bet that explains why he's not coming around," Hattie says. She touches her fingers to her lips because she most likely didn't mean to say those words out loud.

"Hey"—Coral points her way—"you're onto something. I'd notify the sheriff's department tip line or something if I were you. Julian could be a menace to society." Her hand creeps up to her throat. "Come to think of it, if he did kill Glenn, I don't think I'd want Julian or his fancy food around here. The last thing we need is negative attention drawn to this place. Just because Glenn's stubbornness cost him his life, doesn't mean the rest of us should have to lose our livelihoods over it."

"His stubbornness?" I tip my head her way.

"Oh, I—" Coral looks flummoxed by her verbal faux pas.

"She's not wrong," Hattie says. "Uncle Glenn was stubborn to a fault."

Finally. Coral cinches her lips. *Someone who really knew him.*

Can you rescue me now? Cricket yelps as she struggles to break free from the stronghold Coral has on her.

"I'll take her," Hattie says, and Coral is quick to comply. "Coral, who do you think could have done something like that to my Uncle Glenn? Who would have plunged a knife into his back at a family reunion, of all places?"

"I think it's obvious." Coral wraps her arms around her waist. "Julian and Glenn had a heated disagreement. About what, I don't know. But I heard that when our secretary called his restaurant a few days ago, to let them know the number of lunches we would need—something she did every day—she said Julian told her the free meals had come to an end, and that neither he nor his restaurant would be back."

"That sounds a bit harsh." I give Hattie the side-eye and she lifts her brows my way as if to agree. "Well, thank you for your time, Coral."

"Please don't leave." She practically grabs ahold of my hands. "I could give any one of you a great deal on a new car."

"How great a deal are we talking?" Georgie squints at the woman.

"You tell me what your budget is and I'll make it happen," Coral says. *Now that I don't need to run my deals past Glenn, I can wheel and deal and make cars disappear like a magician. That is, until Birdie takes the helm, then it's back to mission impossible as far as getting these buckets of bolts out the door.*

"Fifteen dollars," Georgie says. "And that's my final offer."

And with that, Coral laughs us right out the door.

"Well?" Hattie says as we head back toward the carnival.

"I think we're about to have a nice seafood dinner," I say.

"Woo-hoo!" Georgie leaps and clicks her heels in the air when she does it. "But before we head for the water, how about those corndogs you promised?"

Sherlock barks my way. *One for me, too, Bizzy. If you get me a corndog, I won't tell Jasper you questioned another suspect.*

A laugh bubbles from me. "Okay, fine. Corndogs all around."

Both Muffin and Sherlock leap and howl with glee right along with Georgie.

I link arms with Hattie. "And two funnel cakes for us, to boot."

"Now we're talking," Hattie says as we pick up our stride.

Cricket sighs as she sets her chin down on Hattie's arm. *Once again, we're quickly forgotten.*

Fish looks up at me. *Funnel cake for the felines, too, or be prepared to pay with a spray.*

I wrinkle my nose at Hattie. "Make that three funnel cakes."

The killer will have to pay soon, too.

And maybe, just maybe, we'll be dining tonight with the very man who did the deed.

My phone chirps in my hand and it's a text from Jasper.

I need you to get your mother and her sisters down to the station asap. We've got trouble.

CHAPTER 8

The pets begged to stay at the carnival with Macy and my cousins. They said we couldn't tease them with corndogs and funnel cake and not deliver. And as much as I wanted to chow down myself, my appetite up and left when Jasper sent that cryptic text.

Why would he want my mother and aunts down at the station asap? And what did he mean by *we've got trouble*?

We flew to Seaview, zipped into the sheriff's station, and

made our way to the homicide division. The station is white with a stainless steel design. There's minimal chatter, and an entire infantry of deputies in tan uniforms move to and fro, looking as if they had the weight of the world on their shoulders.

I can commiserate.

I certainly feel weighed down not knowing what surprise lurks around the corner.

"Where's Jasper?" Mom sighs with exasperation.

Georgie nudges me. "Don't you and your hubby have some kind of a sonar to let you know when the two of you are in the vicinity?"

"No, we don't have sonar," I tell her.

"Knew it." Georgie cuts her hand through the air in my mother's direction. "The marriage never took. Good thing we've got Huxley on a blood bond retainer. A guy like Jasper is going to try to take you for all you're worth."

Aunt Birdie's eyes flash with fire. "And she's worth a lot."

Aunt Ruth nods. "She's got that inn."

"And all that land," Mom says, and I shoot her a look for feeding into the matrimonial madness. "Well, it's true. You really should have one of those retroactive prenups drawn up."

"Glenn's prenup was watertight." Aunt Birdie shrugs my way. "But now that he's dead, I'll get my fair share after all." She sheds an easy grin, and both Hattie and I exchange a glance.

She's sure happy about it, too, I say to Hattie.

She nods. "How about this," Hattie says. "Nobody admits to killing anyone while we're standing in the sheriff's station, and that way we can all go out tonight and have a fancy dinner rather than trying to scoop up some serious cash for bail."

"You're onto something, kid." Georgie nods. "We're a team, girls. If one of you offed that man, all of us offed that man. Tonight at midnight—we'll meet at the rocky crags under the bluff, stick a pin in our fingers, and become blood sisters."

Mom rolls her eyes. "We're all related except for you, Georgie. How about we graft you into the fold with a high-five instead? I'd rather not draw any blood."

"Darn it." Georgie snaps her fingers. "But we're still on for the midnight meet-up under the bluff, right? I'll bring the booze."

"I'm in." Aunt Birdie doesn't even hesitate with that one.

"I'll go knock on Jasper's door," I say as I head in the direction of his office.

It takes less than a minute for him to appear. "Sorry about the delay, ladies," Jasper says as he lands a kiss to my lips. "The department secretary seems to have skipped out on us today."

"That's because she's at a carnival making out with my cousin Henry," I tell him.

"Sounds like grounds to get fired to me," Hattie says playfully. "I got canned for less."

"You tell him." I wink over at her. *Although if she gets fired and falls in love with Henry, you might have a brand new nuisance up in Brambleberry Bay.*

Hattie cringes at the thought.

"I can't fire a soul," Jasper says. "You'll have to take it up with human resources. Go ahead and take a seat, ladies." He moves in a couple more chairs, and soon we're all surrounding his desk as he lands on the other side of it.

"Well? What is it?" Aunt Ruth tosses her hands in the air. "The suspense is killing me."

"Are you going to arrest us?" Aunt Birdie snips as if she was angry at Jasper for even thinking about it. "Because if so, I've got to make my jailbreak while I've got a chance."

Georgie taps her. "I knew we should have stopped off at the inn and picked up a bowl of your banana pudding. You'd have every deputy in this place eating out of the palm of your hand."

"Literally," Aunt Ruth says. "I'm getting that recipe before I go back to Brambleberry."

"I want a copy myself," Mom chuffs. "You may be getting away with murder, but you're not escaping Cider Cove without handing the keys to the banana kingdom my way."

"I'd love a copy, too," I say as Mom, Georgie, and Jasper all blink in my direction. "Not for me," I practically hiss. "For the Country Cottage Café. My guests are loving it." I make a face and look to Hattie and my aunts. "I'm not exactly what you'd call a master chef."

Georgie snorts. "More like a master disaster."

Mom nods. "She burns everything she looks at. I'm shocked Jasper hasn't walled off the kitchen in their cottage and put it under lock and key."

"I've considered, it," he says, thumbing through the stack of papers in front of him before looking my way suddenly as if realizing what he's done. "Kidding." He cringes.

"You're too honest," I tell him. "It's true." I glance over at Hattie. "Despite having Baker as my surname, I've been anything but. I'm a catastrophe in the kitchen. I'm shocked Congress hasn't come up with a dozen new laws in an effort to keep me out of it." I sniff in Jasper's direction. "What's the emergency? Is there a break in the case? Did you find the killer?"

"There was an interesting development." He pulls up a

small stack of papers and drums them over his desk. "A letter was delivered to the station today—mailed from right here in Seaview."

"A letter?" My mother grips her throat as if she was about to strangle herself. "What did it say? Was it from the killer?"

Aunt Ruth gasps. "Are they going to kill again? Oh, I don't want to go next."

"Is it from Glenn?" Aunt Birdie looks titillated by the idea. "I bet he faked his own death for kicks. Is he in here somewhere just waiting to jump out and give us the scare of a lifetime?" She cranes her neck to the four corners of the room. "Don't bother," she shouts. "You're better off dead to me."

Mom smacks her on the arm. "Don't be such a nut. Go on, Jasper. Tell us what this is about."

"Actually"—his eyes widen a notch—"Birdie had it partially right. This is a letter from Glenn. Although, as far as I know, he's still in the morgue."

"What?" I lean forward as Jasper hands each of us a copy of the letter. It's typed out with the exception of the signature at the bottom of the page, and that looks to be handwritten.

"To whom it may concern," I read. "Thank you for taking the time to read this. My name is Glenn Pitts, owner of the Pitts Stop. I've given strict instructions to a dear friend of mine to mail this letter should something suspicious ever happen to me. If something suspicious has indeed happened to me, then I speculate I've met an untimely demise. If my death looks like an accident, I implore the sheriff's department to look into it. I am a decent man with no known enemies, with the exception of three bitter sisters I regret having anything to do with."

Mom and her sisters all gasp in unison.

I make a face before reading on. "The Pahrump sisters

have had it out for me as far back as my college days. First, there is Reeann—the one who stole my heart to begin with. I regret how the end of our relationship came to be, but the past is the past and I can't do anything about that now. Then there is Ruth, not the ruthless of the bunch, but I hurt her deeply and she swore she would get revenge one day—and that I would never see it coming."

Aunt Ruth presses her lips tightly and gives a tiny nod of admission to the accusation.

I clear my throat. "And finally, the meanest of them all, my deepest regret on the planet is Birdie Pitts, the one I finally married. Though we had some good days, they were few and far between. She's been after my money from the moment we met. And she's never made that a secret."

"What?" Aunt Birdie balks in protest. "All I ever wanted was a fifty-fifty marriage. Why couldn't we have a joint bank account? Why couldn't I be a fifty percent owner in that dealership of his? We fought about that until the bitter end. The man didn't know the meaning of a true marriage, as evidenced by his loose morals with even looser women. Go on, Bizzy. I'm not saying another word."

Mom pats her on the hand. "You take the high road."

I shrug. "Should I wind up dead, I'd investigate Birdie first. She's a con woman and a liar who will say anything to save her neck. Don't trust her at her word. If I'm gone, each one of those Pahrump sisters needs to be shaken until they spill the truth. I hope this letter never finds you. Glenn Pitts." I pause a moment before reading the rest. "On a side note, head down to the Pitts Stop Dealership and mention that Glenn sent ya. They'll take care of you real good. I wouldn't mind making one last sale myself."

"Oh, for goodness' sake." Mom rolls her eyes. "The man was a salesman right to the end."

Aunt Ruth huffs, "And if he thinks he's sorry he met us, he didn't understand what true remorse was. The Pahrump sisters are ten times sorrier that we ever met him."

Aunt Birdie gives an aggressive nod. "And boy, am I steamed. I wish I could go back in time and slap him a few times before the killer got to their dirty work. I don't even know if I'd get in the killer's way. The man was diabolical. Knowing Glenn, he arranged for his own hit just so he could make our lives miserable one more time."

Both Mom and Aunt Ruth agree with the asinine theory.

Georgie chuffs, "Ain't that a man for you."

Jasper's brows pinch. "I've heard a lot of theories, but that's one I can't get behind. Glenn's dealership was doing well. And apparently, he had an amicable and somewhat pleasant relationship going with a woman by the name of Coral Shaw."

"She's a hoot," Georgie says, and I shake my head covertly at her, but she's not paying me any attention. "We were just hanging out with that hot toddie down at the dealership. It's corndog and funnel cake day in that part of Edison. If you're smart, you'll take your wife back and have a hot date. She owes me a corndog, so you might want to let me tag along for the ride."

Jasper's eyebrows hike as he looks my way. "You went to the dealership to question Coral, didn't you?"

I take a deep breath. "Okay, fine, but we all went as a team. And in my defense, Aunt Birdie wanted to give us all a tour."

Aunt Birdie chokes on her next breath. "What's the matter, Detective? Afraid your wife is going to catch a killer before you do?"

"It's happened before," Georgie says through the side of her mouth.

Jasper flashes those lightning gray eyes my way. "What did you learn?" *If you'd rather share when we're alone, I'm okay with that.*

"No, it's fine." I shake my head. "I think Coral admitted to stealing funds from the dealership."

Mom and her sisters gasp.

"She's the killer," Mom barks.

"I knew it from the beginning." Aunt Birdie shakes her head. "I knew she was after his money. Glenn was a horny toad. What else could a pretty woman like that want from him?"

"I think we should look at the books," I tell Jasper.

Hattie nods. "But there was one more thing. She mentioned that Julian, the owner of Julian's by the Sea, was very upset with Glenn leading up to the murder. And that Julian had a very big secret of some sort."

Jasper sheds an easy smile my way. "I take it we're headed to dinner?"

I nod. "The entire lot of us."

"Okay." He clasps his hands together and his demeanor shifts to a much more somber mood once again. "Ladies"—he looks at my mother and my aunts—"I need you to know that the letter each of you has a copy of appears to have been signed by the deceased. Even though the letter was typed, the signature at the bottom was not. We had a handwriting analyst look at it and compare it to Glenn's signature on several documents we were able to obtain, and it's the real deal. Either someone was an expert at signing his name or indeed he wrote this and had a friend drop it in the mail. Just know that the department is taking it seriously. Birdie, I have a question I need to ask you specifically, so if you'd rather have everyone leave the room, I'll leave that up to you."

"I don't have anything to hide." My feisty aunt folds her arms tightly across her chest.

"Okay." Jasper winces. "When I questioned you the day of the murder, you said you were getting a refill of your banana pudding about the time of the murder."

"That's right," her voice spikes as she says it. *Oh, for goodness' sake, why did I ever say that?*

Hattie and I exchange a glance.

Jasper sighs. "I checked with the kitchen staff. They said there was no refill at the café. Where were you really?"

Aunt Ruth's mouth rounds out. "And why was your T-shirt soaking wet?"

"For Pete's sake." Mom swats Aunt Ruth. "Did you have to go and incriminate her? Jasper might be family, but he's still obligated to uphold the law."

"I'm innocent as a bird, just like my name suggests." Aunt Birdie waves them both off. "I'm sorry, Jasper. I didn't mean to lie to anyone. In fact, I didn't. I was so flustered after confronting Coral that I headed straight for the café thinking it was my bistro, and I was going to get another refill of my pudding. Call it old age or whatever you like, but once I stepped into the café, two things happened. I realized my blunder, and I suddenly had to tinkle."

Mom clucks her tongue. "TMI."

"Well, I did," Aunt Birdie crows. "The air-conditioning was so high the urge hit me fast, and so I bumped into an empty table with a full and very *melted* shake on it. The darn thing tipped over and splashed onto my shirt. I ran to the restroom, did my business, and since I didn't want to look like a slob in front of all my relatives—including Glenn and his hussy—I took off my T-shirt and rinsed it in the sink. And why are we still talking about me? Didn't you hear your wife say that Coral is stealing from my dealership? I say let's nab the little thief."

Jasper's lips purse. "Bizzy, I'll need the receipts of everyone in that café up to three hours before the murder. I need to see if there's a shake that was sold in that time frame. No offense, Birdie. I'm just doing my job."

I pat Aunt Birdie on the arm. "We sell at least fifty a day. I'm sure there will be plenty of shakes to corroborate your story. And you're right, we need to focus on Coral. And maybe Julian. So who's up for a fancy dinner by the sea tonight?"

Everyone in the room lights up at the thought.

Jasper walks us out, and he offers me an embrace as we're about to part ways.

"It looks as if we're squeezing a date night into our investigation, Detective Baker Wilder." He sheds a grin my way. "Julian Richards was on my radar, too. Several witnesses identified him having a tussle with the deceased that afternoon on the cove. He's the guy who I told to leave once Hattie mentioned it looked like he and your uncle were about to come to blows. Julian took off in one direction, and I took off for the cottage to change my clothes. Coral might be stealing, but Julian is still very much a suspect."

"Poor Uncle Glenn had so many things working against him. And that letter?" I shudder. "It's creepy, but very sad he felt he needed to write it."

"Did he write it?" Jasper shrugs. "He could have. Or the killer could have pulled it off in an effort to pin this on your relatives."

"Now that's diabolical. Can't wait until dinner." I land a kiss to his lips and linger.

"And I can't wait for dessert." He waggles his brows.

"*Ooh*, I hope they have crème brûlée!"

"IF THAT'S another way to say *Bizzy in my bed*, then I'm hoping for a double portion."

"Double portion, huh?" I give his tie a quick yank. "Watch it, Detective. I might just make all of your dreams come true tonight."

We split ways, and all the way back to Cider Cove I think about the killer.

All of their nightmares are about to come true. And if the killer sent that letter to the sheriff's department to set up my family, I plan on being their biggest nightmare of all.

They won't get away with Uncle Glenn's murder.

And I sure as heck won't let them get away with framing my family.

CHAPTER 9

*J*ulian's by the Sea is a posh establishment with an old-world charm and just the right hint of new money—lots and lots of money.

The exterior is comprised of stone walls and arched windows. Inside, it's dim, with glossy dark wood flooring and matching furniture, as light jazz music plays through the speakers. There's a small dance floor near the bar with couples dancing cheek to cheek, and the scent of grilled seafood infiltrates my senses as we wait to be seated.

This place is almost packed to capacity tonight, but when I called ahead to find out if Julian would be in tonight—and thankfully he is—the hostess told me we lucked out. It was their slowest night of the week so we wouldn't need a reservation. Good thing, considering we're coming in with nearly a dozen people. Word spread fast, and Winnie and Neelie, along with Hux, Makenzie, Macy, and Juni decided to join us as well. Henry dragged Camila along, and Mom brought Brennan who has both of my aunts enchanted with his adorable accent.

Hattie leans my way. "Your mother had better watch out. Those two have stolen her boyfriend before."

I make a face. "Here's hoping Brennan's life isn't on the line because of it."

Georgie and Juni wiggle and squirm as they seemingly adjust themselves while looking at their reflection in the oversized aquarium housing live lobsters and crabs.

"What are they doing?" Hattie whispers.

"I don't know," I say. "Georgie does like to show off how breezy her kaftans can be. Maybe she's giving a demonstration?" Georgie has donned a black and silver kaftan, and it's the most elegant I've seen yet. She's even got an oversized tote bag to match. "And, well, Juni is wearing an impossibly tight leather dress. It's cut to her thighs but keeps riding up. Maybe she's trying to get it to behave?"

Hattie nods. "And those fishnets she's paired it with look itchy."

Mackenzie steps our way. "They're dancing like that because they've got crabs. That's where those fishnets get you." She sheds a dark smile.

Mackenzie has her chestnut locks pulled back into a twist and she's donned a navy dress that accentuates her baby belly. For the first time, Mackenzie looks painfully swollen. "I'm going to get every lobster in that tank tonight," she says, practically salivating while looking at the wall of seafood where Juni and Georgie are doing their quirky moves. "Actually, I want a seafood tower, Hux," she snips. "Make that two."

My brother tilts his head her way. "I'd stick to one meal, Mack. We'll run by a fast food place on the way home for you." *The girl could out-eat a frat house. Correction, every frat house at any university.* "If we hit too hard with the food, Jasper might want to split the bill."

"Hey?" I nudge him.

"What? You invited us." Hux shrugs, still in his suit from a day at the office.

"Stop being so cheap, Hux," Mackenzie hisses. "Dinner is on Huxley and me," she shouts, and our entire party gives a cheer—with Jasper's being the loudest.

I can't blame him. The average ticket price at this place is sixty bucks. I'm shocked they have two customers, let alone dozens upon dozens.

"And why aren't we seated yet?" Mackenzie snips again. "My stomach is about to digest itself."

Huxley's face goes pale because his wallet is about to get digested.

A waitress shows up, and soon we're threading our way through the dining room on our way to a table by the window. It's already dark out, but the reflection of the moon dancing on the water is mesmerizing.

Macy tugs at my sleeve. "Check out that hottie by the bar."

I glance that way and gasp because the hottie is someone I recognize. "The bald guy with the dark beard?"

Hattie then tugs my other arm. *Macy is talking about Julian! This is perfect. I bet she'll make sure we get his attention. You better believe it.*

"That's him." Macy pulls down her hot pink dress until her bosom is about to bounce out and slap me across the face. "He's got a mischievous look in his eyes that I really can go for. Trust me, I can pick 'em."

"You can pick 'em, all right," I say as we bypass a young couple staring lovingly into one another's eyes.

I can't believe we're at Julian's. The young woman giggles as she looks over at the debonair man with a suit on. *And here I was wondering where my next lobster dinner was coming from.*

I can't believe we're at Julian's, he says a bit more lackluster. *I'm going to have to eat ramen for a month just to work this into my budget. I asked to eat at the burger joint I manage and she laughed right in my face. Here's hoping she says yes when I ask to head to my place for a movie afterward.*

She nods. *And as soon as we're through, I'm heading straight home. I'd hate for him to think my body could be bought for the price of a seafood dinner.*

Hattie shrugs over at me. *I'm rooting for her.*

I nod. *And feeling sorry for his wallet. She's going to be expensive to chase.*

As she should be—I think.

It's mostly couples here tonight.

That's understandable.

This is the kind of place you'd want to bring your date to if you were trying to impress them. That or a birthday, anniversary, or any sort of a special occasion, but definitely not somewhere you'd eat on a nightly basis.

We take a seat at an expansive table. There's a couple

seated to the right of us, who happen to have a cute little boy no older than two sitting in a highchair between them. The mother keeps trying to give him a bite off her plate, and he comically turns his head dramatically from one side to the next.

"Look at that." Mom nudges Brennan on the arm. "Isn't he adorable?"

Brennan coos at the young man.

Brennan still has a swoon-worthy Scottish lilt to his voice when he speaks. He has crimson wavy locks, a ruddy complexion, and is tall and barrel-chested. He works as a host for a local food channel and sometimes does national shows as well.

Who in their right mind would bring a toddler to a fancy place like this? Brennan shakes his head.

"It won't be long now, lad," Brennan pats Hux over the shoulder. "That will be you and Mackenzie with your wee one soon enough."

Mom chuckles. "If the two of you ever want to get away for the night, I will happily watch the wee one for you. Your father and I never took you kids to a single fancy restaurant."

"And it shows," Mackenzie says, knocking Huxley's elbow off the table before flagging down the waitress. "I'll double your tip if you take our orders now and get the food to the table before I dunk my head into one of those lobster tanks and start eating them live."

"What's everyone having tonight?" The blonde with a toothy smile laughs as she pulls out her notepad. *They don't pay me enough. Correction, they don't pay me anything. My tips are on the line. I'd better widen my smile if I want to earn my keep. It's bad enough the food in this place is cooked by a bunch of chefs in training. If I've learned one thing from working here, it's don't mess with a mama-to-be. And this mama-to-be had better make good on her promise to double my tip. But, just in case, I'd better flirt with Lightning Eyes here.* She gives Jasper a sly wink.

Hattie gags and looks right at me. *How are you handling this so coolly?*

I shrug her way. *Lightning Eyes is pretty hot. Besides, he comes home to me at night. It's only fair I let the other women in the world admire him from afar. Except you. You probably shouldn't admire him from any length. That would be weird.*

Duly noted. She laughs my way.

Camila chortles obnoxiously loud at something Henry says, and they both turn to look in our direction.

Jasper expels a breath. "All right, what's so funny?"

"Nothing." Camila brushes him off. "It's just a little inside joke between Henry and me."

Henry nods our way. "Jasper, you're a lucky man to have been with a sparkling gem like Camila, and now my cousin Bizzy."

Sparkling gem? I give Hattie the side-eye.

Ignore him, she says. *That's code for* **I'm trying to get lucky.** *I've met a few of his sparkling gems before. They tend to lose their luster about mid-morning the next day.*

Good to know, I say.

No sooner do we put in our orders than an entire parade of appetizers is shuttled to the table. I'm just about to bite into my Cajun fried shrimp when that cute little toddler starts to scream at the top of his lungs.

"Here we go," Mackenzie says. "It's like I'm being targeted. Wherever I go there's a screaming kid to greet me. It's as if the universe were trying to warn me what the next decade of my life is going to be like." She glances to the ceiling. "I get the message loud and clear."

"Oh, it's not all about you," Camila dares to snip at Mackenzie. "Some of us happen to like kids." She nods to Henry before slithering all over him like a forked-tongued python.

Boy, she's really laying it on thick, I tell Hattie. *If I didn't know better, I'd say she was going for the gold—as in a gold band for her left hand.*

Hattie shakes her head. *It won't happen. Henry isn't programmed for monogamy.*

The kid cries louder, and soon everyone in the restaurant is craning their necks in his direction, giving cutting looks to the poor mother and the father—both of whom seem unfazed by the cries of terror emitting from their spawn.

Geez, someone growls. *Put a cookie in him already.*

Can't they see we're trying to enjoy ourselves? A woman scoffs. *I left my kids at home, hoping to have a little adult conversation. Some people are so inconsiderate.*

Georgie attempts to clap in his direction while clutching her oversized tote bag to her shoulder as if she was struggling to hold it there. Come to think of it, that bag looks unusually bloated. It's as big as Santa's sack. Has it been that size this whole time and I hadn't noticed? It's as if she has two king-size pillows stuffed in there.

"He just needs a little attention," Georgie shouts, and the mother scowls our way. "I had a wee one myself way back when." Georgie smacks Juni on the back as if she were trying to dislodge a chicken bone. "I brought her to fancy restaurants all the time and let her cry it out." She leans a notch their way and nearly falls out of her seat. "Pretty soon management was paying *me* not to eat at their hoity-toity places. It's good work if you can get it. And it buys a heck of a lot of Sappy Meals." She gives a hard wink their way. "You're welcome."

Both the mother and the father look offended at the thought of running such a scheme.

The poor baby screams that much louder and tears spout from the corners of his eyes as if he were a cartoon. His face turns ruby red, followed by a deep shade of plum.

The mother, an athletic-looking brunette, paws at the boy's head. "Crying is okay. It's good for you. Let it all out. Nobody is here to judge you."

The father leans in, dark hair, suit, no tie. "I hear you, son. I will always be here for you. I'm comfortable with your form of expression. I'm here for you while you work it out."

The poor kid's voice hikes ten times as loud, and now he's kicking the table and thrashing his arms around.

Mackenzie squints their way. They're spewing exactly what that new hit parenting book I just bought was touting. If this is the end result, it was another twenty bucks wasted.

"I'm hearing that you need space," his mother shouts over his incessant cries, and the tiny tot grabs ahold of the table-cloth and gives it a strong yank, causing their plates to teeter to the edge of the table and both parents let a few salty words fly.

The little boy laughs up a storm while his parents howl at him to *knock it off right this instant* and he's right back to crying—albeit a weaker far more defeated sob.

"Oh, for Pete's sake," Macy growls over at them. "This is exactly why I'm not having children. They don't let you sleep, and they don't let you eat."

"They don't let you have sex either," Mom offers up far more information than any of her three children were ready for. "It's a miracle I had you girls. Huxley was a pistol right out the gate."

Aunt Ruth elbows her. "No wonder Nathan had an eye for other women."

Mom nods. "He gave them the rest of his body, too."

Mom and both of her sisters laugh at that one.

"At least they're getting along," I say to Hattie.

Camila leans into the table as she looks my way. "Guess who else is getting along?" She lifts a brow to Jasper. "Wouldn't it be something else, if we ended up in the same family after all?"

"It would be something else, all right."

Henry takes Camila on with an amused expression. *Come to think of it, she might not be such a bad starter-wife.*

Ugh, I say, looking at Hattie. *Is it bad that I'm already rooting for the divorce?*

Hattie makes a face. *It could be worse. They could have a couple of screaming children between them.*

They wouldn't be screaming for long, I tell her. *I'm pretty sure Camila would eat her young.*

A plate crashes to the floor and a light applause breaks out.

"That better not have been my dinner," Mackenzie quips.

Macy cranes her neck. *There he is. Mmm, mmm. I think I'll ditch the table of doom and go get me some of that cantaloupe sugar.*

She excuses herself and trots off, but everyone at the table is too lost in the micro-conversations happening to notice.

Jasper leans my way. "She's making a run for him."

I nod his way as we watch Macy work her magic, and in a moment she's cornered him near the bar.

"Why don't we hit the dance floor?" Jasper whispers.

"They're standing right next to it, and I'll buy you a drink afterward."

Hattie leans my way. "I'll get a head start and buy my own drink."

Jasper and I hop up to the dance floor, and no sooner do we start swaying to the music than right next to us appear Camila and poor Henry.

Look at me, Bizzy, Camila says while bubbling with laughter. *I've finally got myself a man just as romantic as Jasper.* Henry twirls her and gives her a dip and Camila squeals like a pig at the trough—at the trough of love apparently.

I frown up at my handsome husband and quickly translate Camila's diatribe.

"For the record, I didn't have a romantic bone in my body until I met you." He tips his head to the side. "How am I doing in that department, anyway?"

"We're still together, aren't we?" I tease as I glance to the bar where I see Hattie laughing and chatting with Macy and Julian. "I'm sorry, Jasper, but I really have to go," I say, sailing right out of his arms and catapulting to the bar.

I glance back, half-expecting Jasper to be on my tail, and to my shock, Camila has wrapped herself around him. Poor Henry.

She's never been one to let a good Jasper go to waste. It's not only her favorite stone, it's her favorite man.

He struggles to untangle himself from her as I turn to my shiny new suspect with a smile.

"Bizzy Baker Wilder," I say to him and note the gold plated nametag on his lapel with the word *owner* just above it. "I see my sister has already thrust herself upon you—to tell you how much we're loving the food, of course."

He belts out a hearty laugh. "Nice to meet you, Bizzy.

Macy and Hattie were both just telling me how much they're enjoying everything."

Julian looks polished in a dark suit with a bright red tie. He has paper-white teeth that glow against his deep, tan skin, and he never seems to lose his smile.

Hattie nods. "He was just telling us about where he gets his lobster from. It sounds as if there's a good chance my dad and his crew could have caught them."

Julian nods. "I do buy local."

Macy growls over at Hattie, *Watch it, cuz. You might be related to me, but that doesn't mean I'm going to play rock, paper, scissors when it comes to giving away my men. And if Julian owns a lobster joint, you can bet I'll do whatever I can to make sure his shiny bald head finds its way onto the pillow next to mine.*

Hattie's mouth opens and closes as if she were going to say something but thought better of it.

Jasper staggers over, breathless. *She's a brute*, he says before frowning my way. *And you might be, too, for disappearing on me. I almost had to draw my weapon.*

A tiny laugh lives in me and I mouth the word *sorry* his way.

"Jasper, this is the owner of the place." I look over at Julian. "Julian, this is my husband, Jasper. My entire family is thrilled to be here tonight."

"Nice to meet you, Jasper. And thank you all for coming. Celebrating something special?" he asks, and I can't help but think how genuinely nice he seems.

"We're having a family reunion," Macy says, gliding her finger along his tie. *What don't Bizzy and Hattie get about this scenario? Can't they see I'm setting a lobster trap out big enough to catch one helluva handsome bald man? I bet he's got enough money, he could fashion a wig out of dollar bills if he wanted.*

"A family reunion." Julian rocks back on his heels. "Nobody appreciates family like I do. Dessert is on the house."

Macy, Hattie, and I coo at the very same time.

"You don't have to do that," I tell him. "But that's very kind. We haven't exactly had an easy go of our family reunion."

Hattie nods. "Our uncle was killed a few days ago, over in Cider Cove."

His eyes widen a notch. "Your uncle wouldn't happen to be Glenn Pitts, would he?"

"That's him," Macy says. "Did you know him?"

I should deny it. He glowers at the bartender as if he had suddenly morphed into my Uncle Glenn. *Although, I'm not sure what the point of lying to these kind people would be.* "I knew Glenn pretty well. I used to cater to his dealership."

Jasper tips his head at the thought. "All the way out in Edison? That's quite a delivery range."

"That's right." Julian takes a breath. "And believe me, it was taking its toll on my delivery van." *And my pocket. But now that Glenn is gone, that entire nightmare is over.*

Nightmare? Hattie's eyes flit to mine.

And he took a hit to his pocket? I muse. *I bet he was cutting Uncle Glenn a deal. Hey? Maybe he bought a car from him?*

"Did you ever buy a car from the dealership?" I ask seemingly out of the blue.

"No, not me." Julian gives a nervous laugh. *After the financial pummeling Glenn gave me, I won't be buying a new car anytime soon. But he's dead now, and I can not only breathe easier, but I might just crawl back into the black again. He closes his eyes a moment. Glenn had to go. It was horrible to see him there like that. But at the end of the day, it was inevitable.*

Inevitable? Hattie shakes her head. ***Bizzy, this man wanted our uncle dead.***

"Julian?" I take a half step closer to him. "Did you see what happened to my Uncle Glenn that day?"

He may not verbalize what I want to hear, but he might just be thinking it.

"I saw him after it happened. It was a tough thing to witness. Nobody deserves to go out like that." *Except Glenn, of course.* "I was there, and we exchanged a few words. He took off, and the next thing I knew I heard screaming."

Hattie lifts her shoulders a notch. "What kind of words did you and Glenn exchange?"

Julian swallows hard. *I can't come out and tell them what was really said—that I threatened to kill the guy if he didn't find some other mark.*

Mark? Hattie and I say at the very same time.

Julian nods. "We talked about the lunch deliveries. We were thinking of switching up the menu a little bit." *As in the menu not existing.* "That was my suggestion, but Glenn made it clear he wanted to continue in the same manner. Some people are creatures of habit with everything, right down to the meals they like to eat." *And that jerk wanted to live off a steady diet of my seafood.*

Hattie, I say. *I don't think Julian was a willing partner in delivering his meals to Edison.*

Edison is pretty far from here, she says. *I wonder why he agreed to it to begin with?*

Money is my guess, Jasper says as if he, too, can read minds. He nods to Hattie and me. *Was I wrong about the trajectory of your conversation?*

I shoot him a wry smile that says *you are good, Detective.*

"Julian?" I bite down on my lip a moment. "It sounds as if you knew him well. What do you think happened that day?"

That's the million-dollar question, Jasper says. *And just to let you know, Hattie, I had him on my list to speak with next. And when I do so officially on behalf of the department, most suspects aren't half as chatty with me as they are with Bizzy.*

The two of you make a good team. Hattie nods his way.

Julian purses his lips.

"Oh, who the heck cares." Macy does her best to swat the three of us away. "Can't you see the man is grieving?" She pulls Julian in close and the guy looks mildly alarmed.

What the heck, he says, sliding an arm around her waist. *She's a babe.*

He lifts his chin my way. "I'm not sure how well you knew your uncle, but he led an interesting life. He has a lot of interesting friends, too. One of which was there that day. A man by the name of Ned Colton."

"Ned Colton?" Hattie inches back as if he tried to deck her. Is this a suspect coming out of left field?

Macy gasps. "*The* Ned Colton?"

"You know him?" I ask.

"Everybody knows him," she snips. "Long flowing curls, big blue eyes, plays the saxophone and sings rock ballads for a living? He's a legend on the bar scene all around Maine." *I've been trying to trap him with my fishnet stockings for years.*

"Wait a minute." I look over at Jasper. "I saw a man with long hair that day at the cove. He was having what looked to be a curt conversation with Uncle Glenn—and then they headed for the woods."

Macy's mouth falls open. "That was him? I guess I didn't recognize him without a herd of women tossing their panties at him." *And to think I had no feelings whatsoever for him in that scenario. I should kick myself for having* the Ned Colton *within my grasp and missing out on the chance to make him mine—for the night, of course.*

Jasper's jaw redefines itself. "Julian, did Ned have anything against Glenn?"

"They were old bar-crawl buddies. Glenn loved to take advantage of people, so he kept mooching tickets to Ned's shows. He started giving them away at raffles, as incentives to close a deal on a few sales, to his employees. Heck, he'd gather an armful of women and head to the shows on occasion. He really enjoyed having Ned in his back pocket. He used to call him his chick magnet."

Poor Aunt Birdie. I sigh.

Julian's shoulders twitch. "After a while, it was costing Ned to have Glenn around. He only got a few comp tickets to each show. The rest was docked from his paycheck at each gig."

"Oh, really?" I blink at the thought. "I bet Ned wasn't too thrilled."

"Nope." Julian laughs to himself. "And what happened next floored even Glenn. One evening Ned had enough. He found out he would be playing a gig that night essentially for free, so he made a beeline to the Pitts Stop Dealership, picked out a cherry of a truck, asked to take a test drive, and Glenn graciously gave him the keys. The guy drove off and never came back. Glenn was fuming. He threatened to sue."

"When was this?" Hattie asks with an amused tickle to her voice.

Julian bobs his head from side to side as if trying to recall. "About two weeks ago. I found out the next day when I brought out the lunch delivery." *I laughed all the way home. The bastard deserved to have every one of his cars stolen in the exact same manner—right under his nose.*

My lips part. If it wasn't clear he didn't care for Uncle Glenn before, it's clear now.

A sharp scream comes from the dance floor, and we look that way to see Camila hopping into Henry's arms.

"My back!" Henry cries out and flops to the floor, spilling Camila onto the floor next to him.

More screaming ensues—this time from our table—and in the blink of an eye, Mom, Aunt Ruth, Aunt Birdie, along with Winnie and Neelie, have all hopped on top of the table and are screaming their lungs out.

"What in the heck," Jasper says as he speeds that way.

"That's what I'd like to know." Julian is quick to follow.

Hattie moans. "I'd better check on Henry."

"Who cares about Henry?" Macy whines. "Even with a bad back, he's probably still getting lucky tonight."

The entire place begins to light up with screams as women jump up on their chairs and look to the ground in horror.

And then I see them—dozens of large brown creatures crawling around the floor in a frenetic frenzy.

"GAH!" Macy howls. "Giant cockroaches!"

"That's our dinner," I shout as I head in the general direction they seem to be streaming from. And once I spot the nexus of this creepy-crawly trouble, I all but freeze. "*Georgie,*" I hiss, only to find her holding that toddler who was screaming earlier as he claps his hands and laughs his head off. "What are you doing?" I ask her.

I'll be honest, I sense a kidnapping charge on the horizon.

"Baby Cheeks and I are freeing our compadres in hostage arms."

"That doesn't make sense. You're not a hostage, and I hope neither is he." I moan as I look at the lobster races seemingly taking place in front of us. "Georgie, you can't free the food," I all but wail at her.

"Says you." She takes the little boy's hand and points at me when she says it.

I'm about to ask where his parents are when I look that way to find them both cowering on their chairs and screaming. I can see where he got his pipes.

Something nips at my ankle, and I let out a harrowing cry before landing on that tabletop, along with the rest of my family.

The wait staff, Brennan, Hux, Mack, and Jasper, along with a small handful of men, all do their best to try to wrangle the beasts, but the panicked crustaceans are proving to be experts at evading capture. If only they were this good at it the first time around, none of us would be in this predicament.

And if I'm not mistaken, Mackenzie is shoving a few into her oversized purse. What are the odds of both her and Georgie coming prepared to engage in a crustacean coup?

The night wears on, and our voices wear out. A few tables give way and send patrons sailing to the floor, and ours gives a good sway.

"Abandon ship, ye lassies!" Brennan shouts our way as the table we're standing on gives another mean wobble. Then in one spastic move, the left side of the table collapses, and every last one of us slides in that direction as if it were a luge. We end up in a pile at the bottom with what feels like a hundred angry lobsters snapping at us as if exacting their revenge on humankind.

More screaming ensues.

The fire department shows up.

An ambulance.

And seventeen squad cars.

Both patrons and lobsters alike run out of Julian's by the Sea screaming their heads off. And just as I hit the fresh night air, I spot Georgie and Juni tossing lobsters from Georgie's tote bag over the pier and into the water.

"She's going to get arrested," I say to Jasper as I nod Georgie's way.

"It would be a relief," he says.

Sadly, this isn't Georgie's first lobster freedom fest she's hosting. I'm sensing a theme with her—and I'm also sensing the fact there won't be any more invitations to seafood restaurants.

The little boy somehow finds his way back to his uber supportive parents, most of the lobsters are freed into the briny sea, and the rest of us head back to Cider Cove a little hungrier than we left it.

Who knew that was a possibility?

Georgie, that's who.

Jasper and I head home and I make all of his dessert-laced dreams come true just the way I promised this afternoon.

It's not such a bad night after all.

I got Lightning Eyes in the end, and I gained a whole new suspect in the process.

Ned Colton, you're next on my list.

CHAPTER 10

*J*ulian Richards did not comp our meals—not that I expected him to. He did, however, add a service charge in lieu of pressing charges against Georgie. But once Huxley took a look at the service charge about to hit his credit card, he begged, rather profusely, for the sheriff's department to lock Georgie up for life.

The next day Jasper left for work early, vowing to dig deeper into Julian Richards, since we weren't able to get him to divulge his secret but were certainly able to ascertain the fact he didn't care for good old Uncle Glenn. Jasper also mentioned he'd try to dig around to find a way to access the financial records from the Pitts Stop Dealership. I let him know that we didn't need a court order to dig into them—we have Aunt Birdie to get us the goods—but he let me know that she doesn't have legal right to the facility as of yet so the long road is the only option.

Maybe the long road is the only option for him, but not for me. Although I'm not digging into any financial records just yet, it is definitely on my to-do list. But not at the moment.

I felt so bad about the fact my family got kicked out of a posh restaurant last night that I hosted an elegant seaside dinner right outside the café this evening in an effort to make up for it. And now that our bellies are full and the sun is setting, we've moved the party down to the beach where I've set up a huge bonfire to accommodate our budding brood.

As soon as it's dark enough, the inn is hosting a movie night under the stars this evening. It's a double feature night. First, we're watching the Disney movie *Moana* for the families staying with us, then switching to *Jaws* for the older set once that's through. I'm sure that will make swimming extra fun for the guests that stay for the second showing. My immediate staff comprised of Jordy, Nessa, and Grady thought it would be hilarious and outvoted me.

I told them playing a movie about a great white in late August would be a perfect way to ruin someone's desire to swim in the Atlantic for the rest of the season, if not the rest of their life, but they brought up the point that almost everyone on the planet has already seen it, so there's that. Next time, I think I'll let the entire staff vote on our movie selections. My guess is they're not nearly as twisted as those I hold close to the vest.

The entire length of the cove is dotted with bonfires tonight, each one with s'mores service available, which has been a huge hit this summer—and it's being offered along with Aunt Birdie's banana pudding, which will have to be a staple at the café because the kitchen staff can't make it fast enough.

A smattering of wonky quilts are set out as families and couples alike watch the sun turn the Atlantic into a tangerine puddle—a reflection of its glory as it sets behind the woods. The Country Cottage Café outdoor grill is working overtime tonight to meet the demand of the hungry guests and the scent of grilled burgers and hot dogs permeates us on this warm summer night.

"Who's up for a good bonfire brownie?" Georgie calls out as she comes dancing down the beach in her deep purple kaftan.

"Bizzy?" Jasper gives me a look that asks far more questions than my name. *I think we know what's in those brownies. Sounds to me she's still gunning to land your family behind bars.*

"I think you're right." I give the scruff on his cheeks a quick scratch before getting up.

Jasper looks unfairly handsome tonight. He's been turning heads all evening, and I even heard both Winnie and Neelie have a few passing thoughts on how handsome my husband is. Winnie said I was living a charmed life and was lucky to have him. But Neelie's mind went straight to white noise.

Essentially, white noise is an emergency kill switch when it comes to mind-reading abilities. It means that person's thoughts have gone wild in the coital sense, so I'm glad I'm not privy to anything in that category.

Hattie felt so bad she apologized. I told her I never hold people responsible for their wandering thoughts. It's a whole different ballgame compared to what comes out of people's mouths. I can't judge anyone for where their mind travels—especially when they have no idea someone has access to them.

Jasper stokes the flames and the bonfire grows six feet, sending a plume of smoke into the sky. With the amber flicker lighting up the night, the woodsy scent of smoke, and the waves crashing down over the shoreline in the distance, it brings back every wonderful summer memory I have ever cherished.

"Georgie?" My bare feet dig into the quickly cooling sand as I make my way around the smoky fire to where my mother, Brennan, Aunt Birdie, Aunt Ruth, and Juni sit huddled, chirping amongst themselves in what seems to be a lively debate about the ethics of having live crustaceans as source food in restaurants. "Did you make these brownies? More to the point, are these your special brownies?"

Before she can answer, Sherlock and Muffin run this way, tongues and tails a wagging.

Georgie made special brownies! Sherlock barks. *Please tell me these have bacon in them and not that special human catnip she likes to ruin them with.*

Georgie lets out a full-on cackle. "I don't need to be a mind reader to know these pooches came for my goodies. Lucky for the two of you, I made a few with bacon. The rest are jam-packed with what I like to call—"

"Human catnip?" I beat her to the punny punch.

"Boy, you really are a mind reader," she says, tossing a few brownies to the dogs that look more like blondies. Thankfully, Georgie understands the fact dogs can't have chocolate in their diets or the first three letters of the word *diet,* itself, might kick into effect.

"Please tell me you didn't use your special medicinal stash of human catnip to fill those magical brownies." I don't know why I asked. I already know the answer.

"Okay, I won't." Georgie shrugs. "But only because you said please."

A hard groan comes from me as she tap-dances her way through the sand and lands in a seat next to Aunt Ruth.

"Fair warning," I tell the eager hands already dipping into Georgie's platter of ooey-gooey goodness. "Those aren't your average brownies. They've been medicinally enhanced," I say the word *medicinally* in air quotes, hoping they'll get the hint.

Aunt Birdie claps her hands. "Georgie, did you make Space Cakes to kick this night off in the right direction?"

"You bet that bee in Bizzy's bonnet I did. Go on and have as many as you like. I've two more batches back at the house. And an entire canister filled to the brim with more of my tingle berry tincture."

"Wonderful," my mother says as Brennan reaches across her and nabs one of Georgie's sweet spacey treats and her mouth falls open as she looks at him.

"Don't blame me for wanting to try one, lassie," he tells her. "You know I'm a fiend when it comes to chocolate."

"That I do," Mom says with a graveled tone. ***And I've used it to my advantage on more than one occasion.*** "Oh, what the heck." Mom snatches up a brownie and moans as she takes a bite. "Wow, Georgie. I can't tell at all that these have been altered."

Juni snickers as she snatches up a handful herself. "But I

have a feeling we'll all be able to tell once you've been altered, Ree-Ree."

"I have a feeling you're right," I say, making my way back to my seat where I find Fish nestled in Jasper's arms and Cricket snuggling in Hattie's lap.

Bizzy, Fish says as she jumps into my lap as I fall into my seat. *Macy is up at the grill, drinking shots with Winnie and Neelie. She says she's going to get them good and schnockered so they can have some real fun.*

"If real fun means hovering over the toilet, they're going to have a blast," I say, stroking my sweet cat's back.

"You're right." Hattie cringes. "Neither Winnie nor Neelie is a big drinker. They can't hold their liquor and have been known to hug a toilet. I can't imagine they'd let her talk them into it."

Jasper leans in. "Have you met Macy?"

Hattie laughs. "The real question is, has Macy met *Neelie*? Neelie doesn't need liquor to turn her world or anyone else's upside down. Let's just say she's an expert at having a run-in with the law."

"Yikes." I shudder at the thought. "I'd warn Macy, but in truth, that's the kind of knowledge that would only entice her."

Muffin barks. *Someone's coming this way.* She cranes her furry little face to the left. *And they're big and furry, and running at top speed! Quick! Everyone take cover!* She quickly buries her head underneath my seat as her furry body shivers beside me.

Jasper leans up. "I hear barking."

So do I, Sherlock says as he jumps and snaps in that direction. *It's them! They're here! Cinnamon and Gatsby are baaaack!*

"Emmie?" I nearly toss Fish into the air as I jump up out of my seat.

Sure enough, Emmie and Leo are headed this way, along with their sweet dogs, and all four of them seem to be wearing ear-to-ear grins.

I waste no time in pulling Emmie and Leo into a group hug. Emmie and I share the same dark hair and blue eyes, and Leo is a tall, dark, and handsome looker.

"I'm so glad you're back," I shout. "I don't care if you were gone for a long weekend. It always feels like a million slow years go by whenever you're away."

They share a laugh at that one.

Gatsby and I feel the exact same way. Cinnamon barks.

Cinnamon is an aptly named cinnamon-colored labradoodle with the cutest button eyes you ever did see. And Gatsby is her male counterpart, a golden retriever who always looks as if he's smiling.

Fish yowls at the sight of them, *Come on, Cricket. These two really know how to race across the cove. They won't get to the crags before us, but they'll put in an honest effort.*

I'm all for a race, Cricket says, jumping out of Hattie's arms.

Muffin dislodges herself from under my seat, and her long fluffy fur is going every which way—think bedhead with sand. *A race? Again?*

Sherlock barks. *That's right. Let's go, Muffin. We need to take down those cats once and for all.*

I'm not cut out for this! Muffin wails. *Don't you animals believe in all-you-can-eat buffets? Glenn said they were the highlight of all existence. He never once made me move my paws in a hurry. I don't think this is healthy!*

The four dogs take off, with Muffin lumbering along with

her hind end bouncing to the right and left. The poor thing isn't really built for speed.

But the cats take off like a bolt of lightning in a blurry streak of fur, and if I'm not mistaken, they've already magically appeared near the crags. These races of theirs are never fair. The cats have it in the bag each and every time.

"Come here, you two," I say as I pull both Emmie and Leo closer to the bonfire and quickly introduce them to my aunts before hauling them over to take a seat near Jasper, Hattie, and me.

"My cousin Henry has a trick back, come to find out," I tell them. "Camila tried to jump into his arms and they both landed facedown on the dance floor. He's up in his room right now being tended to by the same woman who took him out." Both Emmie and Leo cringe. They're more than aware of Camila's antics. Leo knows them best, considering he dated her for quite some time. "And this is my sweet cousin, Hattie Holiday," I tell them. "Just so you know, she happens to have the same talent that Leo and I share."

Emmie moans as she looks to Hattie. "So you're pretty much a disaster in the kitchen, too, huh?"

"Emmie." I chuckle as I give her a playful shove.

"I know, I know." Emmie laughs. "I was teasing," she says as they take their seats. "So Hattie, are you, you *know*..."

"Telesensual," Hattie says it lower than a whisper, and she quickly fills them in on how we discovered we share the same gift.

"That's so amazing." Emmie shakes her head. "See, Bizzy? I've been telling you for years to ignore your mother's ban on all family reunions and get to one."

"I should have listened," I say. "I've missed out on so much."

Leo nods to Hattie. "Well, I'm glad you and Bizzy finally

reconnected after all these years. How did the family reunion go?"

Leo and Emmie have instated a no cell phone rule for their long weekend getaways. All of Cider Cove could burn to the ground, and they wouldn't hear about it until they saw the smoking ruins for themselves.

"You first," I say. "How was the honeymoon this time?"

I hand both Emmie and Leo a bowl of banana pudding off the table next to us and they dive right in before letting out a collective moan.

"Who made this golden delicious treat?" Emmie moans. "And is this your way of firing me?"

A laugh bumps from me. "Aunt Birdie made it, and don't worry. I've been fiercely protecting your position. Aunt Birdie is too busy minding her own bistro to come and take over the café. I've already tried."

Jasper looks my way. "Is it my imagination, or are they evading the question?" He nods to Leo. "All right, what happened this time?"

Emmie spikes her spoon back into her banana pudding. "Fine. But first, I think I owe Hattie a little bit of history."

Leo groans. "It's not my favorite history lesson."

Emmie smacks him on the arm. "Hey, buddy." She laughs. "It happens to involve our wedding."

"Now *that* I can get behind." Leo snatches her hand and kisses it. "Go on, fill her in on the dicey details."

Emmie sags in her seat. "It all started when I insisted on purchasing a dress that was rumored to be cursed."

"Rumored?" I tease. "Hattie, the dress came with a signed affidavit that it was indeed a haunted frock."

Emmie nods. "And since Bizzy refused to talk me out of it,

I purchased it and wore the thing down the aisle—thus the honeymoon from hell that followed suit."

"Emmie," I shriek her name with laughter. "You tell Hattie the truth."

"All right, fine," Emmie says. "Bizzy begged me not to delve into the dark side of wedding couture, but I wouldn't listen. Anyway, the wedding went off without a hitch. That is, if you don't mind a sudden freak storm hitting the reception. Then, on the way to our honeymoon, our car flipped over the bridge, but thankfully we were all right. And in light of the fact, Leo and I vowed to have as many honeymoons as we could squeeze in to make up for it."

"Oh, wow." Hattie cringes. "So, have the honeymoons that followed been all you hoped they would be?"

Emmie exchanges a dark look with Leo. "Well, we bought a new truck after our car was ruined in the bridge mishap, so that was something good that came out of it." *If you like car debt.* "Sorry." She wrinkles her nose. "I still can't seem to control my thoughts." She shrugs. "Our little getaway honeymoons have been fun, but there always seems to be something that goes wrong for us. Once we had two flat tires, then Leo got food poisoning, then last weekend I got stung by a bee on my lip and my face swelled up like a helium balloon, and this time—we got a real whopper."

"What happened?" Jasper's voice is sharp.

Leo takes a breath. "It seems someone opened up a bunch of credit cards in my name about a month ago and they've run them all up. Now I've got creditors looking for the cash they think I owe them to the tune of fifty grand."

"*What?*" Hattie, Jasper, and I say in unison.

"Don't worry," Jasper grits the words out as if they were a threat. "We're taking this to the fraud division. Nobody is getting away with this. Whoever is responsible will pay in every legal capacity."

Leo nods deeply. "That's exactly what I told Emmie."

"I'm so sorry," I tell them.

"You're sorry?" Emmie sinks in her chair. "I never would have blinked in the direction of that dress if I knew the effects were going to linger. I thought all that curse stuff was foolish at the time. And now look who's the fool?" She scoops out another bite of banana pudding. "Let's talk about this case you're working on. Nessa and Grady mentioned there was another murder. Who bit the dust this time?"

"My uncle."

Both Emmie and Leo gasp.

"It's true." I quickly fill them in on Uncle Glenn's untimely demise and give them a rundown of the suspects, including my Aunt Birdie. Not that Aunt Birdie could hear any of the accusations flying over all that cackling they're doing on the other side of this fire. It's nice to know the effects of Georgie's brownies happen quickly.

"The Pitts Stop Dealership?" Leo glances to Emmie. "That's where we bought my new truck. Nice place." He offers a conciliatory smile to Hattie.

"You didn't happen to have a female salesperson sell you that truck by chance, did you?" I ask.

"Nope." Leo shakes his head. "It was some guy named Bill. He gave me a sweet deal, too."

"I'm glad about that."

"Me too," Jasper says. "The two of you deserve a break."

Emmie leans my way. "So who's next on your list of suspects?"

"A man by the name of Ned Colton."

"Ned Colton!" Emmie howls as she slaps her chest. "I love Ned Colton."

"How do I not know about this guy?" I shake my head at my own musical ineptness.

"Don't feel bad," Hattie says. "I don't know anything about him either."

"That makes three of us," Jasper says.

"Four." Leo raises a finger.

"He was singing at a wedding that the café catered last spring," Emmie says. "Jordy came with me to help set up the food, and Ned was doing a sound check so I had a chance to hear him. He's fabulous. He has long dreamy hair and a dreamy velvet voice. And when he sings, you can practically feel—"

"The wrath of a thousand husbands?" Leo teases.

"Something like that." Emmie laughs as she lands a kiss to his lips. "Anyway, I stalk his Insta Pictures account." She pulls out her phone. "Let's see where he's playing next." Her thumb scrolls up and down her screen and her face glows a pale shade of blue in the reflection of the light. "Ah! You won't believe it. He's playing at the Cider Cove Orchard tomorrow night."

I take in a quick breath. "At the Montgomerys' orchard, right here in Cider Cove?" I ask, scooting in to see her screen.

"That's right. It looks as if they're having a dessert competition. It says come on down to Cider Cove Orchard for their first annual Slice of Summer Shindig. Bring your sweetie and something sweet to share with others. Votes will be cast, and the person with the most popular dessert of the night will be awarded a blue ribbon and a yearly subscription to Cider Cove Orchard's jams and jellies of the month club. Don't forget your dancing shoes, the barn is looking spiffy, we've got twinkle lights, and Ned Colton is ready to set the mood for some sweet romance. See you all there."

"That they will," I tell her.

Jasper nods. "Let's hope the crustaceans will get to sit this one out."

"Last night was Georgie's latest and greatest attempt at lobster liberation," I say, filling Emmie and Leo in on Georgie's attempt to free every lobster and crab at Julian's by the Sea. "But on the bright side, she's not in jail and neither is any of the sea life she worked so hard to free."

Emmie laughs herself into a conniption. "Given enough time, I bet good money Georgie Conner is about to top herself."

"I don't know," I tease. "You've still got some lingering effects from that curse. You might just top Georgie."

Riotous laughter breaks out from the other side of the bonfire. And slowly, and I do mean slowly, Mom, Brennan, Aunt Ruth, and Aunt Birdie rise from their seats cackling like a bunch of hyenas. They trip over their feet as they struggle to make their way up the sand and land in a heap of tangled limbs—laughing tangled limbs.

Jasper and Leo spring up to free them, as do Hattie, Emmie, and I—but we only seem to get sucked into their hysterical fervor.

The dogs come bounding back our way with Muffin leading the charge.

I'm the fastest, Bizzy! Muffin barks like mad. *Great news! I beat the cats to the crags twice.*

Fish hops over and mewls, *That's because we saw a rat. Cricket and I had to chase him away. It's what we're programmed to do.*

Cricket yowls, *And the rat had a friend, so we each had our own special mission. Don't worry, Bizzy. We drove them out of here. They won't be back.*

Sherlock barks. *And Cinnamon, Gatsby, and I had to chase after those long-tailed vermin ourselves. You know, to see if we could get the squeaky out.*

Both Hattie and I groan at that one. Come to think of it, I think Leo did, too.

Get the "squeaky out" is something these dogs love to do with their chew toys. As soon as there's a chirp, squeak, or squawk detected in any of their toys, their sole objective in life becomes a mission to disable it. The toys usually last all of ten minutes at most.

And that's how I won the race, Muffin trills. *I'm the fastest of them all. Now if only I could find a buffet to celebrate my victory properly.*

"Hey." Mom manages to sit up in the blob of human flesh we've all melded into. "You know what sounds good right about now? A midnight buffet!"

A collective, yet garbled, cheer emits from the munchie-laden among us.

"*Midnight buffet! Midnight buffet!*" they begin to chant—albeit out of turn and slightly off-key.

Jasper and Leo help us all stagger to our feet.

"All right, everybody," Mom shouts while trying to snap her fingers over her head and nearly pokes her eye out. "Let's do the backyard boogie all the way back to the inn and raid the café!"

"*Raid!*" Brennan shouts before doubling over in a fit of hysterical laughter.

Georgie and Juni start singing *cha cha cha* over and over again as the world's slowest conga line stumbles its way up the sand.

Hattie takes a deep breath as we observe the carnage. "At least there aren't any more bonfires in their path."

"Or large bodies of water," Jasper points out.

"But they're headed for my kitchen," Emmie groans. "I'd better get up there and play sous-chef before they cast a pox on the kitchen staff. Tomorrow night," Emmie says, pointing our way, "you guys are going to lose your minds over Ned Colton. His groupies call themselves Colton's Cuties. And I think they're about to gain a few cute members." She winks our way, and we share a laugh.

A thought comes to me. "Emmie, I almost forgot. Winnie is hosting the craft group tomorrow afternoon in the library. You have to come and meet my cousins."

"Will do," she says as she and Leo take off for the café with Cinnamon and Gatsby in tow.

I glance over to Hattie. "What kind of craft is Winnie planning? Do you know?"

She grimaces a moment. "Let's just say she's been known to pull a quirky rabbit out of her hat now and again. But the good news is, she said she's planning a couple of easy crafts, so one of them is bound to be socially acceptable."

"Socially acceptable?"

She shrugs. "Or in the least, it won't give you nightmares."

"It sounds as if I'm about to get to know Winnie a whole lot better tomorrow."

"Here's hoping you still like her," Hattie says as Cricket and Fish chase one another around our feet.

Hattie says goodnight and takes off while Jasper and I hang out by the fire as *Jaws* plays in the background.

I snuggle up in Jasper's lap. "Tomorrow afternoon, I might be getting to know Winnie a bit better—but come evening,

I'm going to get to know our next suspect a whole lot better, too."

"Here's hoping you don't swoon," he teases.

A husky laugh rumbles through me. "Trust me, Lightning Eyes. I only swoon for you."

"Lightning Eyes? Is that a new nickname?"

"Yup. The hot blonde waitress gave it to you last night, so I thought I'd steal it. You like?"

"I love"—he dots a kiss to my lips—"*you.*"

We soak in the last vestiges this warm summer night has to offer, one kiss at a time. In a few weeks, fall will be here and we'll have to snuggle by the fire indoors.

Summer in Cider Cove is about to run out, and so is the luck of whoever killed Uncle Glenn.

CHAPTER 11

*T*he next afternoon the inn is swarming with guests who are anxious to take part in the crafts session.

I told Winnie the inn would cover her fees for materials, and because the session is free, we're packed to the hilt.

"Hello, class." Winnie waves from the front of the library, and the women who have gathered to participate say a collective *hello* right back.

This room is more of a lending library, with rows of dark

mahogany bookshelves lining the walls and a few stand-alone shelves near the back. It's a spacious room just off the reception counter with a stone fireplace that stretches to the ceiling and a few sofas and wingback chairs for the guests to retreat to with a good book in hand. But since we're in need of a workspace today, Jordy helped me set up enough tables and chairs to accommodate all of Cider Cove.

Jordy Crosby is Emmie's older brother. He has the same dark hair, same bright blue eyes, just about to crest thirty. Fun fact: Jordy and I were married for a little more than a day about a million years ago. Cheap booze and an Elvis look-alike played a part in the misgiving. The marriage was never consummated, and my brother did the legal footwork to untangle us from the mess. Jordy has been working for me at the inn for about five years as the handyman and groundskeeper, and we're more than happy with the arrangement.

Both Neelie and Macy seem to be vying for Jordy's attention as they hold him hostage near the entrance to the room. Neelie is coiling her vanilla locks around her finger as they talk, and she keeps kicking her leg up behind her every time she laughs. She is so smitten.

Hattie chuckles. "She's smitten, for sure," she whispers. "And I think Macy is, too."

I make a face. "She's certainly expressed interest in Jordy before, but nothing has come of it. He's sort of a playboy."

"Oh? So he's basically the male version of Macy."

"You pinned the playboy right on the tail."

Winnie calls us to attention. She looks adorable today in a sunny yellow dress with her dark hair falling loose in waves and a tiny yellow bow pinned just above her left ear.

"Welcome to felt crafting." Winnie waves at those of us

seated in front of her. "I'm Winnie Holiday, and this afternoon we're going to work on two simple projects. The first one"—she pulls something out of the tote bag sitting on the table in front of her and it's cleverly hidden by a small white sheet of fabric—"is a pincushion." She whips off the sheet and the entire room gasps.

"You're twisted, sister," Georgie says. "And I like it."

Winnie stands proud, holding what looks to be a doll's head that has a pink stuffed cushion popping up out of its scalp, and that cushion just so happens to be covered with pins.

It looks wrong. Mom shakes her head at the sight.

Aunt Birdie's upper lip twitches. *I always knew something wasn't right with that girl.*

Aunt Ruth makes a face. "Oh, for goodness' sake, Winnie, show them the other project we'll be working on before they all leave." *I will never understand the amusement she gets from shocking the masses. And did she really have to do that in front of my sisters? Embarrassing.*

Fish and Cricket trot into the room, and Hattie and I scoop them up into our laps.

Fish mewls up at me, *Sherlock and Muffin are working the reception area. You'd think people have never seen a dog before with the way they paw at them.*

Cricket yowls, *Fish and I hid behind the desk. I'm not a fan of grabby hands coming at me. I've been known to bite.* She lifts her head a notch, and I swear I see a proud smile blooming.

"That she has," Hattie whispers.

Winnie sets down the prickly doll's head and holds up something small and furry.

"And for our second project, we'll be working on a felt fox."

The room breaks out into a collective coo as I strain to get a better look at it.

"It's so cute," I say as Winnie holds it my way.

It's a tiny orange fox, no bigger than the palm of my hand, with two little button eyes and whiskers. It has a little white belly and black socks on its feet, and it couldn't be any cuter if it tried.

"Felting is a fun and relaxing pastime. You'll each receive a mounting board"—she shouts up over the murmur of voices—"along with a felting needle that looks like this." She holds up a long needle with a pink handle. "And plenty of finger protectors. I don't want any of you leaving today with bloody fingers. Or, worse yet, missing one. Although it would take a little creativity to achieve that fingerless feat."

Mom swallows a laugh. "Not for you, Georgie."

"Watch it, Preppy," Georgie says. "It might just be your finger that I remove." She leans back to get a better look at my mother. "Hey? Maybe a good crafting session is what our shop needs to help boost sales? What do you think?"

"I think anything that requires a disclaimer about not losing body parts isn't for us," Mom wisely points out. "We're still fielding lawsuits from that Passion Potion disaster of yours."

"We're still fielding lawsuits?" Georgie looks affronted by the thought. "Honey, we need a new lawyer. It's time to give Junior the boot."

Mom makes a face. "We can't even afford the lawyer we have, and Hux is working for free. No, I am not firing my own son."

"Have it your way, Prep." Georgie lifts her shoulders as if she doesn't care. "But don't come crying to me when all you've got on your hands are ten bloody stumps."

Mom rolls her eyes as she looks to her sisters. "Do you see what I'm up against?"

But Aunt Ruth and Aunt Birdie are too busy tittering away to care.

"Georgie"—Aunt Ruth gives her a tap on the arm— "I'm packing you in my suitcase and bringing you back to Brambleberry Bay."

"Not if I steal her first," Aunt Birdie says.

"See that?" Mom shoots a look to both Hattie and me. "They're still trying to take what's mine." She leans in and cups her hand to her mouth. "Little do they know, this time I'd be more than happy to let them get away with it."

"I heard that," Georgie says as she squints. "I'm not letting anyone get away with anything, least of all you. Watch it, Preppy. Two can play at the kidnapping game." She points two fingers right at my mother, and now it's Hattie and me tittering.

A woman whisks by the entry as she walks through the foyer and something about her seems awfully familiar.

"I'd better go tend to my guests," I say. "I'll be right back." I go to get up and Cricket lands a tan paw on my arm.

Not without me. Fish and I need to spend all the time we can together before I leave this Sunday. Take me with you.

"Take *me* with you," Hattie says, and I hitch my head for her to follow.

We step out of the room and toward the reception counter where two of my trusty employees are busy taking care of the guests' needs.

The dark-haired handsome looker is Grady, Fish yowls. *And the dark-haired beauty queen is Nessa. They've been with Bizzy for a couple of years now, right out of college, and she's thankful they've decided to stay.*

"Boy, am I ever," I say. "There's no one better with guest relations."

Fish yowls again, *Grady and Nessa have the hots for one another. They sneak off and smooch whenever Bizzy turns her back.*

I suck in a quick breath before laughing. "I'm happy they're happy."

I'm happy, too. Sherlock lets out a little bark as he and Muffin trot our way. *Grady and Nessa have a secret, and they give me a doggie treat each time they ask me to keep it.*

"What secret?" I whisper in the event Nessa or Grady picks up on the buzzword.

Muffin waddles toward me. *They sneak off into the spare rooms when no one is looking. And when they come out, they give both Sherlock and me a treat for watching the fort.*

Manning the fort. Sherlock gently nudges Muffin's snout.

Who cares about the fort? Muffin snorts. *I just want more of Nessa's special doggie biscuits. No offense, Bizzy, but they don't taste like the sawdust cakes you've been passing on to Sherlock.*

My jaw unhinges.

Nessa and Grady have been sneaking away to the empty guest rooms? And asking the dogs to keep watch over the inn? I think they just lost their MVP slots when it comes to my employees. And maybe their Christmas bonuses, too.

"*Bizzy.*" Hattie shakes her head my way.

Okay, fine. They can keep their bonuses. As long as there's no bad breakup coming down the pike, I'll learn to live with the uptick on housekeeping.

And goodness gracious they had better be calling in for housekeeping to clean up after them.

The counter clears of guests, and I quickly introduce Hattie and Cricket to Nessa and Grady.

"We've met Cricket." Grady gives the tiny cat a quick pat. "It's nice to meet you, Hattie. Sorry about your uncle." He shakes his head. *I told Nessa someone was going to bite the dust that day. It's time to face facts. The inn is haunted by some soul-hungry poltergeist. The only way to stop the menace is to blow up the entire building. And maybe burn down Cider Cove, too. I'm surprised the feds haven't stepped in.*

"Nice to meet you, too," Hattie says as she glances my way. *Sounds like Cider Cove had better watch its back.* "Nice to meet the both of you, Nessa."

"I'm sorry about your uncle, too." Nessa winces. "We're not sure, but we think Bizzy might have broken a mirror when she was a kid—every day since birth."

Grady nods. "A very haunted mirror."

Hattie laughs, but before I can say something, that woman walks by again, backtracks then stops off at the desk. A redhead with a slightly concerned look in her eyes.

"Coral?" I say with a twinge of surprise. I knew she looked familiar. Now I know why. "What can I do for you?"

Hattie gasps as well. *Wow. Perfect timing.*

"Girls!" Coral steps our way in a bright red dress with a wicker hat in hand. "I was just coming out because I left a pair of sunglasses here the day of—well, you know." She glances around as if she didn't want to let the other guests in on the fact it was the day of the murder. And believe me, I appreciate that.

"We have a lost and found bin right behind me," I say. "What did they look like?"

"Yellow sunglasses. They're a pair of Fantastiques, so I'm a bit frantic."

"Whoa." Nessa steps over. "Fantastique?" Her eyes grow in size. "I hear those can set you back a cool ten grand."

Ten grand for sunglasses? I glance to Hattie and she wrinkles her nose.

Not happening in my lifetime, she says.

Mine either.

Grady quickly opens up the cabinet and emerges with a pair of yellow sunglasses.

"Oh, thank goodness!" Coral snatches them back. "Fantastique, indeed." She winks over at Grady. *Geez, he's cute. A little on the young side, but what the heck, I could be his sugar mama. And boy, would I like to take him over my knee. But then again, he's probably thirty. I can't guess anyone's age anymore it seems.* "Thank you." She nods his way before sighing. "I showed up an hour ago and retraced my steps. I must have run up and down the cove. I dug all around the café, behind it, along with the wooded side of the building. I even dipped a toe in the water." She shudders as if it were the last thing she wanted to do. "Anyway, I'll be seeing you around. If you're interested in a car, I'm still willing to give you the deal of a lifetime."

Hattie bumps her hip to mine covertly. *I've got an idea.*

"Come back to the inn this Saturday," Hattie says brightly. "We're having our end-of-summer celebration."

"Oh, right," I say. "There will be fireworks and a band. It's going to be epic."

"But most importantly," Hattie leans into the counter, "we're hosting a tiny memorial gathering for our Uncle Glenn. The entire dealership is invited. Would you mind helping us spread the word? Saturday at six."

"There will be food," I tell her.

Coral croaks at the thought. "And more of that banana pudding? I've been dreaming about it ever since that day."

"That's the dessert of the night," I say.

"Yay." She does an odd little dance. "I'll see you girls there.

And I'll tell everyone at the dealership as well. Ta-ta!" She takes off with a wave.

Fish mewls, *Don't look now, Bizzy, but I think Grady and Nessa are getting ready to find an empty guest room.*

I glance over, and sure enough, Grady and Nessa are whispering sweet nothings into one another's ears. Or judging by those wicked grins blooming on their faces, very naughty nothings.

I give Fish's head a quick scratch.

Emmie heads this way with an entire cart filled with individual glass bowls of Aunt Birdie's banana pudding.

"Did I miss the crafts session?" Emmie pants as if she were racing to get into the library. "I thought I'd come bearing dessert. And I want to meet your cousins."

"You didn't miss anything," I tell her. "And you are going to be a hit with my cousins *and* the guests in the room once they see that cart full of banana pudding."

Hattie nods. "Try not to be afraid of the dolls with pins sticking out of their heads."

Emmie's mouth opens and closes. "I'll do my best."

She takes off, and I look to Hattie.

"Brilliant move inviting Coral to the cove. I'll call and invite Julian. And later tonight we can invite Ned. That way, if we have any other questions we need answered, we can pick their brains."

She nods. "But tonight, we dance. It does sound romantic, dancing in a big old barn on a hot summer night."

"Ooh, I should extend the invite to my room thieves." I tick my head toward the new lovers among us.

"The Montgomerys' orchard is having a dance tonight," I tell Nessa and Grady.

Sherlock barks. *The orchard? They allow pets! We're coming, Bizzy. Just you try to stop us.*

"You're welcome, too." I reach down and give Sherlock a pat as both he and Muffin gather around my feet, so I reach back and hand them both a doggie biscuit.

Sherlock gobbles his right up, but Muffin sniffs and prods it with her nose.

When in Rome—even if this version of Rome has questionable taste in food, she quips before chomping it down.

I toss down a couple more. Rome is a generous place after all.

Both Grady and Nessa exchange a glance as they ponder the idea.

"You should come," I encourage them. "A big rustic barn? All the free dessert you can eat? It's going to be a little bit of summer magic right here in Cider Cove. I'll even get your shifts covered."

"Oh!" Nessa dips her knees as she moans with delight. "Dessert and *dancing*? I'm dead," she squeals.

"Dessert and *dancing*?" Grady moans. "I'm dead," he parrots but with markedly less enthusiasm. He twists his lips over at Nessa. "All right, I'll dance. But just the slow songs."

"Are there any other songs?" she teases as she gives his cheek a pinch.

"Get ready to get your groove on," I tell Hattie. "We're going hunting for a killer tonight."

No sooner do I say those words than an entire herd of women stream out of the crafts room holding prickly looking doll heads, and it looks like a parade of horror.

A couple of children shriek in fright.

Sherlock and Muffin bark at the spectacle.

And I can't help but think it looks like a very dark omen.

Whoever killed Uncle Glenn is about to have a pin stuck in them.

And hopefully, Ned will lead us right to the pincushion.

Hattie nods. *That is, if he's not the pincushion himself.*

CHAPTER 12

The Cider Cove Orchard glimmers like a jewel in the night. The enormous red barn is festooned with enough twinkle lights, both inside and out, to ensure you can see it from space.

All of Cider Cove has shown up for the festivities, and the owners of the orchard, the Montgomerys, have gone all out to create an elegant yet homey affair. People are gathered in clusters just outside the barn, and intermittently you can see dogs and cats woven between them. The Country Cottage Inn might have achieved accolades for being the most pet-friendly resort along coastal Maine but, for the most part, all of Cider Cove is welcoming to the furry among us.

I see Candy. Sherlock barks and jumps with glee as he points west with his snout.

"I see her, too," I say. And just past her, I see Macy with a glass of lemonade in her hand, talking to a man at the entry to the barn.

Muffin barks and yipes. *Oh, I adore Candy. Can Sherlock and I go see her? I promise not to bite or nip at anyone. Although if I'm offered a sweet treat, I won't decline it.*

"Decline it if it's chocolate," I say, bending over and straightening the ponytail that sits straight up on her forehead. "Gosh, you're cute." I give her furry face a quick kiss. "Watch over Sherlock, would you?" I whisper that last part to her, but Sherlock gives a spirited bark regardless.

I heard that, Bizzy. I promise I won't do what I did the last time I was here.

"Thank you," I tell him before standing and looking at Hattie. "The last time we were here, he took off and had a great time in the orchard."

Jasper sighs. "He didn't show up for six hours. We thought he was dead in a ditch."

"The fire department was involved." I shrug. "And a search team, a hundred strong. He got a little turned around, then took a nice long nap—so the part about the ditch wasn't all that off."

I could have sniffed him out in three minutes, Fish mewls. *But I was back at the cottage taking a nap of my own and couldn't be bothered. I knew we weren't getting rid of him so*

*easily. It was just a month after Jasper and Bizzy got together,
so none of us were all that invested in him anyhow.*

"Fish Baker Wilder." I give her a little squeeze while laughing. "You behave yourself tonight, too. Stay close to the barn and don't leave Cricket's side. We don't want to form a search party for you, too."

Fish gives my cheek a lick before springing down to the ground. *I'll be perfectly safe. In fact, I'll be checking in on you once in a while to make sure you're not in danger. Come on, Cricket. You won't believe the number of field mice we'll get to chase. We'll work up an appetite then sneak over to the dessert table.*

Ooh. Cricket hops from Hattie's arms and lands next to my feisty feline. *I live for whipped cream.*

We split ways from the pets as we follow the crowd toward the lively barn.

The earthy scent from the orchards mingles with the balmy night air. That, coupled with the stars hanging low over Cider Cove, puts me in a dreamy summer night's mood. There is something intoxicating about the ease of this season. The moon, the stars, the warm night air, it's all working together to cast a spell over our sleepy seaside town.

The orchards are spread over a vast acreage, located just past the inn and to the north. Apple orchards take up most of the land, but they have pears and plums on the property, too.

They sell everything from fresh eggs, to fudge and honey in their gift shop. And apparently, they're diving into the jams and jellies of the month club as well. I make a mental note to pick up a subscription for a few people on my Christmas list —maybe all of them. Finishing my Christmas shopping in August could earn me a medal.

But tonight it's not the gift shop that's bustling—the over-sized rustic barn is where the action is.

Throngs of people swarm the property as the string lights up above cast a soft glow over the land. A dirt walkway, with patches of grass, creates a walkway that leads to the oversized structure where all of humanity seems to be funneling into.

Soft rock music emanates from inside the barn as the sound of a man's voice hitting a high note rings out smooth as velvet.

"I bet that's him singing," I say to Hattie as we walk as a group toward the barn.

"Wow, he's good. I can see why he has the masses swooning."

Mom arrived earlier with her sisters to make sure Aunt Birdie's banana pudding was here on time to be entered into the competition. Neelie and Winnie drove over with us. Camila is bringing Henry. And Emmie and Leo gave Georgie and Juni a lift.

We step into the barn, and it's as if we've been transported to a wonderland. More string lights crisscross overhead, along with rustic chandeliers that look as if they're made out of enormous tin wheels. Bales of hay are strategically set about, and people are snapping pictures of themselves in front of them.

Couples dance in the center of the room, and all around them friends are congregating in small groups chatting and laughing. The entire right side of the barn is lined with tables covered with every dessert imaginable, and there are several refreshment tables dedicated to fresh lemonade and coffee. Up front, there's a makeshift stage with a band belting out a decent tune that keeps the bodies swaying. But it's the long-

haired singer squinting as he croons away that has my immediate attention.

Jasper leans in. "We'll corner him during his break. In the
meantime, let's hit the dance floor."

My mouth opens as I look to Hattie, and before I can feel
bad about ditching her, Jordy Crosby swoops in wearing a
dress shirt and jeans, along with those hooded lids of his and
devilish smile, and asks if Hattie would mind hitting the
dance floor with him.

"You bet," she says as they sail off. *Geez, he's good-looking.*
With a face like this and a body like that, this night is showing
some real potential. I wonder how he'd feel about a long distance
thing? And that's just like me. In my mind's eye, I'm planning
my wedding, and all this poor guy did was commit to a little
fancy footwork.

I'm pretty sure that commentary wasn't meant for my
prying mind, but it shows exactly how alike Hattie and I
really are.

"She's already planning the wedding." I bite down on a
smile as Jasper lands us on the dance floor and pulls me in
close.

"Speaking of weddings." He nuzzles his cheek to mine and
the scruff on his face tickles me. "Our one-year anniversary is
coming up in a month."

"Has it been a year already?" I pull back a notch and take in
this gorgeous man before me. The dark hair and the dark
scruff on his cheeks only make his eyes glow all the more.
"Our lives together are going to evaporate if it keeps going by
this fast." I lean in and take in a lungful of his spiced cologne.
Jasper has donned a blazer and a dress shirt for the occasion,
along with a pair of jeans and dark boots. He couldn't look

more scrumptious if he tried. "Every day I think to myself, how did I get so lucky?"

"I'm the lucky one around here." He takes a playful bite out of my neck. "After that disaster with Camila, I thought I'd be a bachelor forever—and happily so. But then I met you—running into the Atlantic to save your poor cat."

"And then you ran in to save *me*." I bat my lashes at him. "I'll never forget how you looked, soaking wet in your suit. You were so ornery afterward, I wanted to have Jordy kick you all the way to the curb, but something in me knew better."

"That's because I was a guest of the inn." His chest bounces with a quiet laugh.

"And then that homicide happened."

"And you would not stay out of my case no matter how many times I asked you to." His brows pinch together. "Come to think of it, we're still having that conversation."

"Not tonight we're not. Tonight we're going in as a unified front." I pause a moment. "With Hattie and me doing all the talking. You just sit there and look pretty."

"Did you say pretty?"

"All right, we can go back to Lightning Eyes." A dark laugh rattles through me. "Play your cards right, and there might be a spontaneous roll in the hay in it for you."

His brows bounce. "You are on fire tonight, Bizzy. I'll take you up on that offer, but this place better watch out. We've been known to cause a little spontaneous combustion."

A ruckus comes from our right, and we turn to find Georgie charging into the barn in what looks like one of her wonky quilts fashioned into a coat.

"All right, listen up!" she howls and manages to garner the attention of half the people in the enormous structure—no small feat. "I've got a wagon full of wonky quilts half off, just for the night." She tears open her coat and exposes us to dozens of colorful bottles sitting in miniature pockets sewn to the inside. "And if you're feeling like you need to have an old-fashioned roll in the hay, I've got a permit to thrill. Passion Potion is back and better than ever before. I'm running a two-for-one deal good for the next hour only. A woman like me has to get her groove on, too, you know. There's not a dance floor my tired dogs haven't hit. Watch out, gentlemen. I've been known to put the *woogie* in boogie. Gimme your shimmy, and we'll see where the night goes from there. I've got a couple of gallons of Passion Potion sitting in the corner of the room to prove it. Let the romance commence."

A swarm of people surrounds her at once, and she leads the charge to her stash of wonky quilts and deadly potions. I'm half-afraid of where this night will lead.

"*Hey!*" Macy bellows as she stomps over to the swarm encircling Georgie. "You want romance? I've got candles up the wazoo in the back of my car." *I was just about to junk a boatload of evergreen candles that smell more like body odor than they ever do anything remotely related to pine. What the heck. If Georgie has created a marketplace, who am I to eschew a room full of wallets?* "Buy one, get two free!" *Of course, that one will set them back thirty bucks, and I'll still pull in a hefty profit. I knew the gray granny would come in handy sooner than later.* "I'm setting up shop in the corner by the selfie station!"

"Watch it, sister," Georgie growls. "That's my corner you're trying to jab your high heel into."

The two of them take off in haste, and the entire mob follows along.

"Who knew Georgie was such a good saleswoman?" I say as I spot my mother and Brennan speeding out of the barn. "I take it my mother isn't impressed with Georgie's business acumen."

"That's because your mother still has the aftertaste of all those lawsuits thrown at her last month."

"Hux said he took care of them. Here's hoping Georgie left out the stinging nettle in her Passion Potion this time."

"I'd say let's live dangerously and give it a go, but I don't want either of us screaming for the wrong reasons tonight."

"Or any other night."

Camila and Henry crop up beside us, looking into one another's eyes and giggling to themselves. Camila has a short black dress on and Henry's donned a spiffy suit. I'll admit, they look decent together. But Henry is so handsome he'd look decent with a barracuda wrapped around his neck—a prime example of what's taking place now.

"Jasper." Camila looks up with a ruby red grin.

I'm not offended by the lack of acknowledgment. Whenever Jasper is around, that's all she sees.

"It seems I've finally found someone suitable to replace you with, in my heart." Her false lashes flutter a mile a minute.

Her heart? Henry inches back and sheds a contrived smile at her. *And here I thought she was on board with a little fooling around before I took off for home this weekend.*

"Oh?" I ask, amused, knowing full well how Henry feels about it. "So the two of you will be doing the long-distance thing?"

Camila rolls her eyes. "Oh, dizzy Bizzy. Don't you ever leave that motel of yours? Brambleberry Bay is only an hour away. Jasper's commute to Seaview is forty-five minutes in heavy traffic. Surely I'm worth an extra fifteen minutes to my honey pot." She lands a kiss to Henry's cheek.

"Honey pot?" I can't help but give a crooked smile to my poor cousin.

Henry winces. "It has to do with—"

"Nope." Jasper lifts a finger. "No need to extrapolate." *We don't want to know.*

"No, we don't," I whisper. "Well, we're happy for you both." A tiny laugh springs to life in the back of my throat. "Enjoy the dance."

Jasper swings me in the other direction, and I spot Nessa and Grady holding one another tightly, sniffing around one another's necks. Emmie and Leo are here doing the exact same thing. Emmie catches my attention with a wave before pointing to her left.

I suck in a quick breath at the sight. Just a few feet beyond them, Hattie and Jordy are having what looks to be a rather flirty conversation.

"Look at that," I whisper to Jasper. "I recognize that look on Jordy's face. He's thinking about going in for the kill. Can't say I blame him. Hattie is beautiful."

"And she's out of his league. Jordy isn't what I'd call a repeat offender, if you know what I mean."

"Yup," I say. "He's the king of one-night stands. Hattie deserves better. Too bad, though. If Jordy cleaned up his coital act, they might have had a shot."

The song ends, and to our surprise, Mackenzie lumbers up to the stage wearing a bright red dress that's cinched off just under her bosom, making her baby belly look twice as massive as it normally is.

"Oh, wow," Jasper moans. "You don't think she ate Hux, do you?"

My chest vibrates with a laugh. "No, I see him to her left, but it does make me wonder if there's just one baby floating around in there. I'm thinking she's capable of a litter. On the bright side, if there was more than one, she might offer to give it to us."

He chuckles. "Don't be surprised if she offers to give us the one she's carrying. She's not exactly maternal."

"And shockingly, my brother is going to have to be the one to step up to the plate. They're due next month. Grab the popcorn. Things are about to get interesting."

"Hello, one and all." Mackenzie's voice swims around the barn in an echo. "I'm Mayor Woods, and I want to welcome you to the Slice of Summer Shindig tonight. Thank you to Melissa and Topher Montgomery for inviting us all down for some dancing and dessert. It's wonderful for us to gather as a community and kick up our heels together. Speaking of which, I want to take a moment to invite every single one of you to Summer by the Sea out on the cove this Saturday at six. There will be some seaside fun and fireworks as we say goodbye to this hellish season that makes our ankles swell and causes us to retain enough water to pull the West Coast out of its drought. And if one more obnoxious moron out there asks if I ate my husband, I'll skewer you and land you on a spit myself."

Topher Montgomery scuffles with Mackenzie for the microphone before giving a nervous laugh to the crowd.

"Thank you, Mayor Woods. And thank you to Ned Colton. While he's taking a short break, we're going to hit some country music for a bit. Remember to cast your votes at the dessert table. Most popular dish of the night gets a cool grand, a blue ribbon, and the best prize of all—a subscription to the jams and jellies of the month club. And for those of you who want to walk away a winner, there's still time to purchase your very own subscription. Don't forget the holidays are just a hop and skip away. They make great gifts for yourself and others. Enjoy your night."

"I've already mentally purchased one for everyone we know," I tell Jasper.

"At ninety-nine bucks a pop, I hope we don't know many people."

"Wow, ninety-nine bucks? They've got to be making a killing," I say just as I spot Ned Colton heading for the makeshift bar near the stage. "Speaking of killing, I think it's time to slay our suspect—proverbially speaking, of course." I give his tie a quick tug as we head in that direction.

"Wait for me," Hattie calls out as she scuttles over to join us. "You're not going in without me."

Country music blasts through the speakers a touch too loud, and the crowd on the dance floor gets right back to hopping and bopping.

"I'm surprised you're not otherwise occupied," I tease.

She glances to the ceiling. "I'd lie, but word on the street is you read minds. Boy, Jordy is a good kisser."

"You kissed him?" I stop cold to gawk at her.

"What? Don't judge. I'm leaving in a couple of days. I've got to work quickly."

I make a face. "Just don't let him lead the charge. Jordy isn't exactly into working up to the good stuff. He likes to round out the bases on opening night."

"*Oh.*" She cringes. "So that's what all that white noise was about." She wrinkles her nose. "He's out front as we speak, stocking up on Passion Potion. Now I feel like I led him on."

Jasper's chest bucks with a laugh. "Don't worry. His money won't go to waste. Rumor has it he goes through a bottle a night."

"Not with me, he won't." Hattie looks disappointed as if she wouldn't have minded all that much if it *was* with her.

We belly up to the bar where Huxley is ordering a couple of drinks, and standing on the other side of him is Ned Colton speaking to Mackenzie.

"This is perfect," I whisper to Hattie. "We'll wiggle our way into the conversation seamlessly."

She nods. "Let's be subtle about the murder."

Hux turns our way and grins. "Well, if it isn't the three detectives."

He bellows it out so loud Ned turns to take a look at us, as does Mackenzie.

Hattie elbows me. *So much for subtle.*

"How's the case going?" Hux looks to Jasper. "Or should I ask you, Biz?" He nudges Ned in the ribs. "My kid sister is the number one homicide detective this side of the Mason-Dixon line."

Jasper looks ready to deck him. *Is he purposefully trying to get under my skin? Or is this his way of ruining your investigation?*

"Most likely a little of both."

Mackenzie scoffs. "Ned, this is my sister-in-law, Bizzy, her husband, Homicide Detective Jasper Wilder, and my husband's cousin, Hattie. They're on a hunt for whoever killed their uncle. Maybe you heard about it? A slaying at the cove last weekend?"

Wonderful. I sag as I look to Hattie. *There goes any hope of pumping him for information.*

She gives a long blink. *And if he is the killer, he'll do his best to throw someone else under the bus.*

"Nice to meet you all," Ned says, and his voice is just as smooth and silky as it was while he was belting out a tune.

His hair falls to his shoulders in golden soft waves. He has big green eyes, a slightly crooked nose, and a pointed chin that gives him an elf-like appeal. Apparently, a very sexy elf, judging by the way women are tittering and stealing glances his way.

"Believe it or not, I knew Glenn," he offers up without any prodding.

"How's that?" Jasper asks. *I may as well pretend to play a part in this investigation.*

Ned offers a somber smile. "Glenn and I went way back. Old college buddies. We did the bar scene for a while. He had a real successful dealership out in Edison that I'd stop by once in a while. Well, you know all about the dealership." A tiny smile curves on his lips. *Still remember that shocked look on his face when I drove my baby off the lot. He had to be kidding when he threatened to sue. If I totaled up my losses, he would have owed me two sets of wheels. He's lucky I didn't sue him.*

"You frequented the dealership?" Hattie looks mildly pleased. "So you probably knew the staff. I just spoke with Coral Shaw. She's really broken up about Glenn's death."

"She should be. Once her husband went away, I'm pretty sure Glenn stepped in as her sugar daddy. That's one high-maintenance woman. I can spot 'em a mile away. I've always had good radar when it comes to that kind of thing."

Something about the way he's judging her doesn't sit well with me.

"Maybe so," I tell him. "But she said she's been the top salesperson for six months in a row. It sounds to me she's earning her own keep."

Thank you, Hattie says. *Why is it when a woman has nice things people assume a man purchased them for her? Coral works hard for her money—and not in some sick, perverted way.*

She leans his way. "Did you know Julian Richards? Apparently, he catered to the dealership—seafood lunches. A good friend of my uncle's, I guess."

"Ha!" Ned doesn't bother to hide the fact he contests the idea. "Julian and Glenn were anything but friends. I'm sorry to speak harshly of your uncle, but he had a hard time holding onto any real friendships."

"What happened with Julian?"

He glances over his shoulder where Mackenzie and Hux are whispering between themselves.

"This is off the record, Detective," he says, looking right at Jasper. "Glenn told me about a year ago that he found out Julian wasn't paying his employees—at least not many. He's got a kitchen full of interns, and he has the waitresses and bartenders work for tips. Apparently, the ticket prices of those meals warrant enough of a tip for most of those kids to stick around. But if the labor board found out what he was up to, he'd be forced to pay up, and you better believe his staff would lawyer up. Glenn said Julian was just keeping his head above water."

"That's terrible," I say.

Jasper blows out a breath. "And I'm guessing Glenn blackmailed Julian into offering a seafood buffet each and every afternoon to his employees."

Ned nods. "It kept Glenn quiet and made him look like a hero to his employees. Anyone who really knew Glenn would know it was a farce."

Aunt Birdie mentioned something about him being a cheapskate, I say.

Yup, Hattie agrees. *And sadly what I knew of him, blackmail wasn't off the table.*

Jasper leans in. "Ned, can I ask when you saw Glenn last?"

"That day at the beach." He glowers into the crowd. *I'm not about to tell this cop that I drove a truck off the lot and wouldn't give it back.* "We talked about spending a little time together soon." *With our attorneys present. But I'm not offering up that detail either.* "He was in a hurry to get back to the party." *He said I was lucky that he had other business to tend to or he'd call the sheriff's department to the scene and have me arrested.*

"Ned"—my voice comes out a touch too pleading—"who do you think killed Glenn that day at the cove?"

"Tough call." His brows hike a notch as he shakes back his golden locks. "It could have been Julian. My guess is, he's relieved to have Glenn off his back. And then there's that ex of his. Glenn painted a psychotic picture of the woman who I'm guessing is your aunt." He mouths the word *sorry.* "And, of course, Coral. She's money-hungry, that one. Maybe she got him to sign some huge insurance payout if he died? I can't figure out why he'd be worth more to her dead than he is alive. But"—he slaps Jasper on the back—"that's for you to figure out. Or maybe it's you ladies who will crack the case." He gives a condescending wink our way. "I'd better hit the stage. That's why they pay me the big bucks." *And thankfully, Glenn's not here to ruin it for me.*

He takes off just as Sherlock and Muffin come barking this way.

Bizzy, Jasper—Sherlock barks and tugs at Jasper's pants—*the dessert is disappearing. Quick, there's a plate of biscuits I've been working to overturn all night. I could use a little help, buddy.*

Muffin barks up at Hattie and me. *If you saw those biscuits, you'd be desperate, too. How about tossing a cookie or two my way? I can't stop drooling while thinking about them.*

"How about if we cut a deal?" I say as I give her furry head a quick scratch and straighten her ponytail in the process. "I'll sneak you a cookie if you let me ask you a few questions later?"

Deal! Muffin barks at the top of her lungs. *Let's go, girls.*

She leads the charge, and we join the masses as we load up on a platter's worth of dessert. I may or may not have slipped Sherlock and Muffin the lion's share of strawberry shortcake biscuits.

Once we're through grazing our way through the sugar field, we each cast our votes—for Aunt Birdie. Not only because she's our relative, but because her banana pudding wins hands down. And as busy as we are chowing down on delicious desserts, Georgie and Macy seem to have scooped together quite the crowd as they demonstrate their wares.

Georgie is spraying down what looks to be two shirtless men with a hot pink bottle of what I'm guessing is her Passion Potion. And Macy has a table full of lit candles flickering like a sea of stars as women fight to snap up a trio of candles to call their own.

Mackenzie takes the stage again.

"Drumroll, please," she says, and the drummer is quick to oblige. "The winner of tonight's dessert competition who will be going home with not only a blue ribbon and a cool grand, but also the coveted jams and jellies of the month club subscription is—Birdie Pitts!"

A riotous applause breaks out and just as quickly a collective gasp as a majority of the crowd twists and turns as they look toward the ground.

"What's going on?" Hattie says as Jasper groans.

"Bizzy." He points straight ahead just as a blur of two seemingly sweet cats darts by.

They're on the chase! Muffin barks. *They found a squirrel and decided to take his squeaky out.*

They'll never do it, Sherlock says. *Many a dog has tried, and many a dog has failed. The cats don't stand a chance.*

"Let's hope he's right," Hattie says. "The last thing we need is Cricket or Fish getting bitten, or worse. *Cricket,*" she calls out, but it's too late.

The squirrel hops up onto the first of the dessert tables and darts right down the middle of it, then onto the next dessert table and onto the next. And hot on his heels are Fish and Cricket, a little less elegant than their vermin furball in arms. They flip platters and tip cakes, and even manage to send an entire tray of those strawberry shortcake biscuits to the floor—which in turn sends every canine in the room bolting in that direction. Sherlock and Muffin were no slackers. They were the first on the scene.

"No, no," Jasper says, taking a step forward then freezing as we watch the squirrel leap onto the table laden with Macy's candles. The bushy-tailed fiend sends about a dozen candles sailing into the air, and what he misses, Fish and Cricket send flying themselves.

In one quick whoosh, that entire corner of the room ignites in flames, and soon people are screaming and running for the exit—because evidently, the roof is on fire now, too.

Jasper, Leo, Hux, and Henry work alongside the firemen, who just happen to be here tonight as guests, and they make sure not a soul, furry or otherwise, is left behind.

We watch as a crowd as the entire barn goes up in flames like a tinderbox.

Georgie speeds this way with her wonky quilt coat pulled up over her head.

"Georgie Conner!" Mom riots as she and Brennan race this way. "You did this! You knew that Passion Potion is comprised of oil. You were practically hosing down the barn with a flammable liquid. I'd better find Huxley. Here's hoping he can talk the Montgomerys from suing the very souls out of our bodies." She and Brennan take off just as Macy trots this way with her little furball, Candy, by her side.

"This is all your fault," Macy and Georgie say to one another at the very same time.

"Me?" Macy balks. "You brought the flammable love potion to the party."

"And you brought the heat." Georgie gives her the stink eye. "Just like you always do, Blondie."

The whoop of a squad car shrills through the air and the seizure of red and blue lights flashing sends the two of them freezing solid.

"I need to get out of here before they arrest me," Macy shouts as she scoops up Candy in a herculean feat.

Let's blow this joint. Candy barks, and I can't help but note the distress on her furry little face. *I don't look good in orange.*

I'm guessing she's heard that phrase a time or two from my living-on-the-edge-of-the-law sister.

Georgie links an arm through Macy's and they sprint for the parking lot.

The barn burns to cinder right before our very eyes.

The Montgomerys seem genuinely glad that everyone made it out of there alive.

The rest of us head back home with our bellies full of sweet treats and our feet a little worse for wear.

Ned Colton put his voice to good use on more than one

occasion tonight. He certainly painted a picture about both Julian and Coral.

Julian was being blackmailed.

Coral was a gold digger, and maybe a thief by her own admission.

Ned seems to have gotten what he wanted from my uncle with that truck he drove off the lot. Not sure there's too much of a motive there.

Now all there is to do is see how much money Coral may have stolen from my uncle, if indeed she stole a dime.

Someone killed Uncle Glenn, and I bet they thought they had a good reason to do it.

But they were wrong. Dead wrong.

And soon they'll be dead in the water when it comes to their freedom.

They're living their last days of freedom, just the way Uncle Glenn was living the last days of his life.

And the two of them will forever have one thing in common.

The rest of their lives as they know it will have come to a sorrowful end.

CHAPTER 13

"I can't believe you're leaving in two days," I say to Hattie as we stand in the foyer of the inn with my mother, her sisters, and a rattled, yet oddly, cackling Georgie. It's after midnight, and we've just arrived home from the barn burning—and how I wish I weren't being literal.

"What are you doing?" Mom taps Georgie on the arm. "You're acting like an insane person."

"*Shhh.*" Georgie lands her forefinger to her lips. "You'll

blow my cover. I'm laying the groundwork for an insanity defense. Hux says they've got a case if they want to sue. Word to the wise, I'd hide the silverware and jewels before the feds move in on us."

"*Us?*" Mom shrills. "It would figure you'd take me down with you."

Hattie chuckles softly. "I'm really going to miss this. Although, here's hoping no one ends up in the slammer. So what did you think about our conversation with Ned?"

I shake my head. "Julian had the most at stake. The only thing not wiping Coral from my radar is what she said—or more to the point, what she didn't say."

Hattie nods. "I know. She said something to the effect that Uncle Glenn was wrong—the cars *didn't* sell themselves. And now that he was gone, she could continue to suck the funds out of that place."

"That lying snake in the grass," Aunt Birdie growls as she struts this way. "So she *was* after his money. And she's stealing from the dealership! *My* dealership. How do we prove it? I want that hussy tossed in the pokey. No more banana pudding for her. Serves her right for stealing from my Glenny."

Her Glenny? I'm not even going to touch that.

"Aunt Birdie, do you have access to the accounting at the dealership?" I ask. "We can go to my computer right now and poke around and see what we find."

"No, but I can take us to the dealership and we can go through *their* computers," she offers.

Aunt Ruth balks at the thought. "As if the staff there is just going to let us breeze in and start going through their financials. I'm pretty sure they'd call the sheriff's department on you, Birdie. You don't have the keys to the kingdom just yet."

"Says you." Birdie digs around in her pocket and comes up with a keychain full of keys in every shape and size. "I've got the keys to the kingdom right here. I've had the spare to the main entrance on my keychain for years. And if we go now, there won't be any pesky employees to ask me to leave."

"Ooh," Georgie growls. "A little breaking and entering after hours without any of the actual breaking and entering. I'm in, Toots. Give me a minute to take off my bra. I'm a bit more agile when I'm not being held together with rubber bands."

"It's after midnight," Aunt Ruth says to Birdie. "We're all held together by rubber bands at this hour."

Aunt Birdie looks to Hattie and me. "I'm in if you girls are."

"We're in," we say together.

"And just like that, the six of us, in addition to two lightning-quick kitties and two biscuit-loving dogs, all pile into my mother's minivan and head for Edison.

If Coral Shaw is a thief, we'll find out about it tonight.

And once she's crossed off our suspect list, all arrows will point to Julian Richards.

Maybe, just maybe, this case and the Pahrump Family Reunion will come to a close at the very same time.

❖❖

"IT SURE IS creepy here at night," Hattie says as we do our best to slink our way through the abandoned dealership. Half the lights are on, but it's such a cavernous building it still feels pretty dim in here.

Sherlock and Muffin chase one another around a yellow sports car on display in the showroom while Fish and Cricket slink right along with us as we head to Glenn's office.

As soon as our furry menagerie heard we were headed out on a secret midnight mission, they jumped into my mother's van with us.

Thankfully, Jasper is still at the Montgomerys' orchard trying to help deal with the aftermath. There's no way he would approve of us breaking into the Pitts Stop, even if we did have the key.

Hattie lifts a brow my way. *And even if Aunt Birdie was able to correctly guess the code to the security system?*

A tiny laugh bounces from me. *That only makes this twice as diabolical.*

"Here it is," Aunt Birdie says as we all pile into Uncle Glenn's office.

It's a boxy room filled with bookshelves along the back wall, an oversized wooden desk that takes up most of the space, a couple of chairs, and the metallic scent of despair.

Okay, fine. It doesn't smell like despair as much as it smells like an old gym locker. But in Uncle Glenn's defense, he's been out of the office for the past week.

Aunt Ruth sniffs around. "I bet he's got a stash of potato chips here somewhere."

"Potato chips, Ruthie?" Mom balks. "How can you think of food at a time like this? We're about to access sensitive financial records that none of us have any business looking at—least of all the wife Glenn worked to ostracize from this place."

"I can't help it," Aunt Ruth hisses. "I think I still have the munchies from the other night." She looks over at Georgie. "Tell me this isn't some long-lasting effect from those magic brownies of yours. I've already gained ten pounds since I've been to Cider Cove."

Aunt Birdie snickers. "That's because you can't keep your

hands off my banana pudding. But let's face it, Ruthie. My banana pudding is worth a couple dozen pounds of padding."

"She's not wrong," Mom says, poking around at the bookshelves lining the far wall. "These books all look so dry. *The History of the Automobile? Manifold Destiny?*"

"Crack one open," Georgie says. "I bet that's where he hides all the girly magazines."

Hattie lifts a brow. *I'm half-afraid she's right.*

Aunt Birdie waves me over to Uncle Glenn's massive wooden desk.

"Go on, Bizzy. Do your thing," she says, and I fall into the giant leather chair.

The computer is on, so I tap the keyboard, but instead of spilling all of Uncle Glenn's secrets, a request for a password pops up on the screen.

"Shoot," I say. "Any idea of what it could be?" I ask Aunt Birdie, and she quickly taps at the keyboard until the computer relents and lets us in.

"You did it," Hattie says just as Fish and Cricket land on the desk next to me.

Fish mewls, *Bizzy is a whiz at looking through other people's financial statements and telling them where they're going wrong—and she can even detect a little thievery. But when it comes to her own inn, she can't see the profit, loss, or the thieves. That's a direct quote from Jasper, and you know it, Bizzy.*

I frown over at my precocious kitty. "She's right," I mutter. A green triangular app catches my eye. "Here is it," I sing softly. "This is a sister software to the one I use. It's the lower tier model, so the monthly fee is cheaper."

"That's my Glenn." Aunt Birdie clucks her tongue. "Cheap to the bitter end."

Hattie scoots in close. *And that's why he had no problem blackmailing Julian.*

I nod. *I think the killer is either Julian or Coral. And this might just narrow the field down to one.* "Let's see what we can find out," I say. "I'll look for some common discrepancies. Believe it or not, I've actually dealt with this in the past on a case or two."

Mom huffs, "Bizzy has solved so many cases, I'm surprised the sheriff's department hasn't recruited her."

Georgie gravels out a husky laugh. "Oh, hon, sorry to break it to you, Preppy. But the sheriff's department doesn't suffer amateurs. They've probably put a hit out on her already. I wouldn't stand so close to her, Hattie. And Fish? If you're smart, you'll hang back a few feet yourself. They're aiming for the heart. I'd hate to see you lose one of your nine lives."

"What about me?" I balk at the wonky quilt-loving granny.

"It's been great knowing you, kid. I'll make sure Jasper and his new wife have a big glossy picture of you at their wedding."

"Gee, thanks," I say as I tap into the accounting software. "Okay, I'm in."

"What are you looking for?" Aunt Birdie leans in.

"Anything out of the ordinary."

There are four categories: payroll, inventory, sales, and marketing expenses. I dive into each and every one of them and can't find a thing that so much as makes me blink.

"All of the expenses are rhythmic." I sigh. "Which usually means things are going as expected."

Hattie scoops up Cricket. "In other words, nothing out of the ordinary."

"Nope." I shake my head in dismay. "I went back as far as two years."

"I don't get it," Aunt Ruth says as she peers over my shoulders. "You said that Coral mentioned something along the lines of sucking the funds out of this place."

Georgie nods. "I bet he knew she was doing it. That's why she stuck him with a blade. It was him or prison. How many people here think she made the right choice?" Georgie raises her hand and we all stare at her for a moment.

"Oh, what the heck." Aunt Birdie raises her hand.

"*Aunt Birdie*," Hattie hisses.

"I'm kidding," she grouses as if maybe she's not.

Fish mewls, *Are you sure Aunt Birdie is off the suspect list? We might want to revisit that.*

Duly noted, Cricket says. *We'll go over all the suspects once we're through.*

"You bet we will," I whisper.

I twist my lips at the screen as a file labeled *employees* catches my eye, so I click into it. Rows of names populate the screen, and I quickly scroll through them.

"There's Coral." Hattie lands a finger next to the woman's name, and I click on it.

"It's a sales record," I say. "Huh, that's strange. It says she sold a car in December, but the other months have a zero in them."

"That can't be right," Hattie says. "Coral mentioned she was the top salesperson for the last six months."

"Maybe Glenn was slacking when it came to filling out the roster?" I quickly click out and click into several other employees' files, and they've each averaged one or two cars a day. "If Coral's sales record is true, I don't know why she'd stay on."

"Then that settles it," Mom says. "The two of you must have misunderstood her. I thought it was fishy that she copped to stealing from Glenn. Not only does she hardly know you girls, but the one thing she did know was that you were related to Glenn. It made no sense."

I glance up at Hattie. "I don't think we misunderstood her. And she specifically said she was sucking the funds out of *this* place."

"I bet she's stealing office supplies," Aunt Ruth says.

"Or coffee," Mom points out.

"I bet that was it." Aunt Birdie snaps her fingers. "Heck, I'd steal coffee from this place, too. In fact, let's grab all we can and get out of here."

"Birdie, you own this place now," Mom squawks. "We're not stealing from you."

"Oh, come on, it's not officially mine yet. Let's teach Glenn one last lesson for old times' sake."

We head out and raid the employee lounge, purging it of a few coffee pods, creamers, and a handful of teabags before rounding up Sherlock and Muffin and heading back to my mother's minivan.

Hattie and I end up in front of my cottage while Mom drops her sisters off at the entry to the inn. Jasper isn't home yet, so I invite her to hang out for a minute and go over our dwindling suspect list. The stars are out in full force, and the heat is pulling the scent from the night jasmine.

"So we're down to Julian?" Hattie asks as we sit on my porch for a moment. We're both holding our sweet kitties as their eyes grow heavy.

Julian? Muffin scuttles over and sits at our feet, that ponytail on top of her head is slightly askew. *I really liked him. Every time he came to the dealership, he brought a special treat*

—a thinly sliced piece of filet mignon. And he always said he'd rather I eat his food than Glenn. That's why he gave me the very best cut.

"That was nice of him." I give her a lengthy pat on her back. "Everyone loves you, Muffin—including us."

"Especially us." Hattie leans in and plants a kiss on the top of Muffin's head, inadvertently squishing Cricket until her eyes bulge.

Cricket lets out a squeal as she leaps from Hattie's lap. *Apparently, she loves you enough to turn me into a bookmark.*

She hops onto the step below us, and Fish joins her.

Fish lashes Cricket with her tail. *You don't think Julian did it, do you?*

I don't think that man could hurt a fly, Cricket mewls.

Sherlock barks. *Those lobsters we helped to free would beg to differ.*

Mmm, Muffin moans. *Bizzy, you wouldn't happen to have any lobster and butter on hand, would you? Julian always made sure I had a healthy bite before he made up a special plate just for Glenn.*

"I bet he made a special plate for him," I muse. "Sorry, kiddo. I'm all out of lobster, and the café is closed for the night."

"Well, Aunt Birdie didn't do it," Hattie says.

"And Ned seemed satisfied with his new truck and the fact Uncle Glenn won't be stealing tickets to his show. Not quite a motive."

"I don't think so either." I sigh. "And there was no proof Coral stole a dime. I'll tell Jasper our findings once he gets home."

A pair of headlights shines our way as Jasper pulls into the driveway.

Hattie says goodnight to us both as she and Cricket head for the inn.

"Julian, huh?" Jasper says as I wrap my arms around him. I just spilled everything Hattie and I have gleaned at his feet. "I'm not thrilled you went to the dealership, but I'm glad it wasn't technically breaking and entering. You're improving."

I give his ribs a tweak and he bucks.

"All right." He laughs. "I'll deep dive into Julian tomorrow. I'd hate to shut down his place out of the blue and put the wait staff out of work, even if they are working for tips. I'll talk to a few people at the sheriff's department on how to go about this without compromising the homicide investigation."

"Sounds good." I hike up on my tiptoes and give him a kiss. "Ooh, you're smokin'—and I mean that in the literal sense."

"The good news is, the Montgomerys said insurance would cover the cost of a rebuild. They're not going to press charges against your sister or Georgie. As for me, I need to take a shower." He backs up, and his lids hood over. "Care to keep me company?"

"I thought you'd never ask."

We head inside, and Sherlock, Muffin, and Fish curl up in their respective beds by the hearth while Jasper and I get squeaky clean and a little down and dirty.

Summer is coming to an end, and so is Uncle Glenn's murder investigation.

Now it's just a matter of time before Julian is brought to justice.

I'm pretty sure they won't be serving steak or lobster where he's going.

And to Julian, that might just be a fate worse than death.

CHAPTER 14

$\mathcal{S}$aturday evening rolls around as quickly as a summer storm. But there's not a cloud overhead this evening. It's panning out to be the perfect summer night, one of the last of the season.

Yesterday, my cousins and aunts hung out with Mom, Macy, Georgie, and me on the beach. We sipped frosty drinks while slathered in coconut-scented suntan lotion, read books, and took naps intermittently. It was the perfect summer day. And I'm hoping tonight will be the perfect summer evening. But I won't lie. Having a crowd congregating around the inn makes me uneasy at this point in my life.

There have been far too many homicides, far too many bodies I've inadvertently stumbled upon. Emmie might think her marriage is cursed, but I'm starting to wonder if I'm the one the bad juju is attracted to.

The cove is bustling with bodies. The café's outdoor grill is sending a plume of smoke into the sky as the scent of grilled burgers and hot dogs lights up our senses.

Henry and Camila are sprawled out on a wonky quilt by the shoreline and looking all that much cozier by the minute.

Mom, Aunt Birdie, and Aunt Ruth are tossing a bright green Frisbee to one another, and both Sherlock and Muffin are doing their best to steal it.

Well, isn't this a show? Fish mewls in my arms. *Sherlock doesn't like sharing his toys.* She lashes Cricket with her tail as Hattie holds her. *Things will get interesting once Sherlock realizes that the sole reason they're tossing that disc isn't to land it in his mouth.*

Cricket vocalizes what sounds like a laughing yowl. *You're lucky to have Sherlock in your life. He's so entertaining and strong, and handsome and...*

And annoying. Fish is right back to lashing Cricket with her tail. *I can't believe you've fallen into his trap. What sucked you in? His dry wit or his incessant need to sniff out bacon?*

Cricket purrs as she sighs his way. *It was those big brown eyes. How do you stay sane? He's out of this world irresistible.*

He's out of this world, all right, Fish growls. *And who's spreading rumors about my sanity? I haven't had that for the last two years. Coincidently, the exact amount of time Jasper and Bizzy have been together.* She takes a moment to give me the stink eye.

Muffin snatches the Frisbee from Aunt Birdie. *I got it! Did you see that, Bizzy? I took it right out of her hands.*

"Good girl." I give her a whoop for the effort.

"You mean *feisty* girl," Aunt Birdie says, giving Muffin a hearty scratch. "You just think you're too cute with your ponytail and sassy swagger. Well, you're right." She laughs as she chucks the Frisbee a few feet over, and Muffin catches it again.

No fair, Sherlock shouts.

Fine, you freckled cutie. Muffin does her best to toss the Frisbee his way, and Sherlock is quick to nab it. *Now go on and toss it back to me. Maybe the humans will get the hint and find their own toys to play with.*

Mom chuckles. "Something tells me they don't want to share."

A white fuzzy pooch comes bounding down the sand. *Wait for me!* Candy calls out. *Macy says I need to get my energy out before bedtime. I bet I can throw it twice as far.*

Candy dives for the flying green disk at the same time Sherlock does and a snarling fest breaks out.

Told you so, Fish mewls, and if I'm not mistaken, there's a twinge of satisfaction in her voice. *Now his true colors shine.*

She wasn't off base with her accusations either. Jasper and I love to spoil both of our pets with toys, and Sherlock does love to hoard them.

Hattie leans my way. "I'm the same way with the toys, and so is Cricket."

"*Bizzy,*" Macy hisses while traipsing through the sand as

quickly as that little black dress she's wearing will allow. "Control your beast. *Candy, play nice!* Remember what I said about saying please and thank you." Macy shakes her head my way. "She's new at all this manners stuff. She was basically raised by wolves before she came into my life." She cranes her neck past me. "Hey, is that Ned Colton setting up on stage?"

I turn around, and sure enough, it's the long-haired crooner who helped fill in the blanks regarding Julian's secret.

"It sure is." I glance to Hattie. "Why don't we say hello before he starts?"

"You do that," Macy says, tugging down her dress as she scopes out the crowd. "I see a couple of hotties by the shoreline who look as if they want to get naughty. Wish me lick."

"You mean *luck*," I say as she takes off.

"I mean lick," she shouts back. "*Sheesh*. Hasn't having a pet taught you anything?"

She's got you there, Fish teases. *Now let's catch up to our old suspect.*

Cricket settles into Hattie's arms. *I bet this is where the real show begins, Fish. Hattie was up half the night, tossing out theories about all of the suspects—Aunt Birdie included. She said she might be moved to look the other way if Aunt Birdie is the killer.*

Fish mewls her way, *Bizzy said the same thing. But then she insisted justice must be done. Georgie was right. She's going to throw us all under the bus one day.*

"I am not." A laugh trembles from me as we thread our way through the crowd. "Jasper is finishing up with a few things at the sheriff's department, but he should be here in about half an hour. A few departments are working together to bring Julian down. He was so nice, I almost feel sorry for him."

"I don't feel sorry for him," Hattie says. "He may have

plunged a knife into Uncle Glenn. And he doesn't pay his employees."

They get tips and street cred, Fish meows.

"Street cred?" Hattie laughs as she looks to my sweet cat.

"That's right," I say. "I guess once they've done their time, he gives them a glowing review and they can go out and get a real job that actually trades currency for their time and talent."

Fish mewls, *That's what Jasper told us. And Muffin has nothing but nice things to say about him. Something smells fishy to me, Bizzy, and it's not my name.*

"Something smells fishy to me, too," I say as I look to Hattie. "But I just can't pinpoint what."

We funnel our way through a mob of people and wave to Ned just before he hits the stage.

"Good luck tonight," Hattie tells him, and he sheds an easy grin her way.

Here's hoping there's a double meaning to that. He waggles his brows at her. *I should probably have my agent rent me a room here at the inn for the night. I'll want to jump on her as soon as I jump off the stage. I have a feeling it's my lucky night, indeed.*

Hattie scoffs. *You'll need more than luck for that to happen, buddy.*

"I'm glad to see you here," I tell him, although after that internal diatribe, it's more or less a lie. "This evening is sort of doubling as a tribute to my Uncle Glenn."

He winces as he looks out at the ocean. "I feel bad for the guy. He wasn't a terrible person. Yeah, he had his flaws, but who doesn't? I'll dedicate a song to him tonight. One of his favorites." *We were good friends for years. He wanted tickets to my show. He wasn't only a fan, he was proud of me. He told me that time and time again. And all I saw was what his actions meant to my bottom line. To steal that truck from him was low of me. The guy didn't even press charges. Yes, he was angry—but he was a true friend to the bitter end. I wish I could have been there for him when he needed me most. I would have loved to have caught the killer just before they did him in.*

"Thank you." I give a mournful smile. "My uncle would appreciate that." *And the fact he truly misses him and wishes he could have stopped the killer—*I glance to Hattie—*makes me think we can completely rule him out.*

Hattie gives a solemn nod. "If you're able to, we'll be just down the beach with Uncle Glenn's widow and the staff from the dealership. She's going to say a few words, then we'll light candles."

It's true. And surprisingly, it was Aunt Birdie's idea to say a few things and light candles in his memory. Muffin was grateful that such a kind woman would honor Glenn.

"I will," he says, squinting in that direction. "The staff from the dealership, huh?" *I'm surprised there's a staff at all from what Glenn said. A scandal like that could taint a person just by association.* "I'll see you ladies later." He winks over at Hattie. "Listen carefully, darlin'. There just might be a special dedication to you as well." *That always cinches the deal.*

Not tonight. She winks back.

He hops on stage, and I pull Hattie to the side.

He's a greaseball, Fish mewls. *I didn't like the way he was looking at you, Hattie.*

Cricket roars, *I didn't need to read his mind to know what direction it was headed in. If he comes anywhere near you tonight, I can't be held responsible for my actions. She whips her tail toward Fish. Have you ever scratched an eye out? Any tips on how to accomplish this best?*

"Whoa." Hattie laughs. "Don't worry. I'm not falling for any of it." She leans in hard. "What the heck was he talking about when he mentioned the scandal at the dealership?"

"I don't know, but he said it could taint a person by association. It doesn't sound good."

The music starts up, and true to his word, Ned dedicates his first song to Uncle Glenn. A song called "My Time in the Sun," one that he said was Uncle Glenn's favorite.

We start to head back to where our family is congregating just down the cove when Fish straightens in my arms.

Isn't that Sherlock and Muffin? she yowls.

Cricket gasps. *And they're playing with the killer. I bet he's plotting to annihilate them, too. We should hurry.*

Walk slowly, Bizzy, Fish says. *No need to trip and hurt yourself.*

"Very funny." I crane my neck in the direction they're looking and spot a bald man with a dark beard playing Frisbee with Sherlock and Muffin down by the water. "Let's go."

"We should play it cool," Hattie pants as she says it. "Although, I'll be honest, my blood is boiling just looking at him. Uncle Glenn didn't deserve what he got."

A warm breeze licks at our faces as we separate ourselves from the burgeoning crowd. And the noise from the gathering fades just enough to be replaced by the roar of the ocean.

"Julian," I say as I force a smile. "How are you? I see you've found my dogs."

"You're taking in Muffin?" He looks a bit surprised. "I'm glad she's found a good home."

"Thank you. I'm more of a temporary portal, but I haven't

even tried to look for someone close to my uncle to see if they want her. I've grown pretty attached to her myself. They'd have to be the right person. But I'm glad to keep her forever if need be."

Muffin barks my way. *Thank you, Bizzy! I know whatever happens, it will be the right thing. I know you wouldn't send me to the wolves. That's something Coral threatened a time or two when I begged for a bite of her food.*

Fish's ear twitches. *Are the wolves looking for a dog to call their own? Perhaps we could see if they're interested in Sherlock?*

I frown down at her a moment before getting back to the task at hand.

"Julian, thank you for coming out. I'm sure my uncle would have appreciated it."

"Oh, he would." *Under one circumstance.* Julian tosses a quick glance to the ocean. *If I brought enough food to feed everyone at his memorial service. Half the staff attacked me when I showed up, wondering why I'm leaving them high and dry at their lunch hour.* "Your Uncle Glenn certainly had a way about him." *And that way was to explicitly get his way. Glenn Pitts was a blackmailing jackass who I'm glad isn't around to bully anyone anymore.*

Hattie takes in a sharp breath. "You hated my uncle, didn't you, Julian?"

It's clear Hattie is far more emotionally sensitive here than I am.

Fish pats me on the chest. *It's too late to stop this train, isn't it?*

Sherlock gives a soft woof. *Jasper asked me not to let this happen. He said to hold you ladies off until he arrived.*

Cricket gives a sharp meow. *Nobody can hold Hattie back*

when she's worked up. But don't worry. She can hold her own. I've seen her go toe-to-toe with her sisters. Even her mother always says that Hattie needs to get the last word. And Henry once said he wouldn't want to be caught in a dark alley with her if he was on her bad side.

Julian's chest pumps with a dry laugh. "I didn't hate him. I felt sorry for him. The guy had a dealership plagued with troubles. He was bleeding employees. He did what he had to keep them. As a business owner, I can respect a man who tries to save his own business any way he can." *Even if it meant blackmailing me into oblivion and almost costing me my business. The man was a menace from top to bottom, but I don't expect these innocent doves to realize that. Nor will I be the one to break it to them. The guy is dead. I'm more than satisfied with the fact he's no longer here to torment me.*

Hattie's mouth falls open. "You're not sorry in the least he's gone because he was coercing you to supply his employees with pricey meals from your restaurant. How dare you show your face today. You're not only glad he's no longer with us, you know your way around a butcher knife, don't you?"

He inches back, eyes agog and mind blank as a cloudless sky.

"I don't know what you're implying, but I didn't kill your uncle. Yes, we had an odd arrangement when it came to catering to his dealership, but I came to the cove that day to let him know there would be no more deliveries. I'm restructuring my business model, and there was no more room in it for him." *And to think he said he would send customers my way in exchange for the fact he was robbing me.* He shakes his head. *He knew darn well that I wanted nothing to do with his customers. His online reviews should have tipped him off.*

"Wait a minute." I look right at him. "My uncle was having

trouble with something at his dealership," I say, hoping to pull the right answers out of Julian. "He wanted to give his employees an incentive to stick around. That's why he hired you." At least I learned that much in the last half hour. "Julian, do you know why my uncle was having a hard time keeping customers?"

He jerks as if I struck him. *I don't want to be the one to tell these girls why their uncle's customers hated him. And I'd bet good money one of his customers came to the cove that day and shoved a knife in his back, just the way Glenn did to the hundreds of people who came to him looking for a vehicle.*

Hattie and I exchange a covert glance.

So much for pinning Julian as the killer. Hattie sighs.

"Look"—Julian picks up the Frisbee and gently holds it in front of Muffin until she clamps it between her teeth—"he had some serious problems with his staff. If you want to know more, I suggest you talk to Coral Shaw, one of his salespeople." *If I remember correctly, he pegged her as his biggest problem. He said he should have gotten rid of her rather than taken her to bed. He knew he had a nuisance taking him down from the inside, but boy, was he fuming when he found out it was her. He was about to take his case to the FBI, and no sooner did he tell me that just last week than he ended up dead.*

"What do you know about Coral?" The words speed out of me so quickly it sounds like one long word.

He cocks a brow. "Nothing really. I think Glenn mentioned her husband went to prison six months ago or so. Not sure for what." He bends over and gives Muffin a quick pat. "I'll see you ladies around." He takes off, and both Hattie and I pull out our phones in haste.

"Coral's husband went away to prison?" Hattie says as we both race to look up reviews on the dealership.

Muffin barks. *He did. Glenn said that Roland Shaw was a lying sack of bull weed.*

"Roland Shaw." I nod, looking him up instead. "Thank you, Muffin."

Hattie and I gasp at the very same time.

"You first," she says.

"Roland Shaw was indicted on wire fraud charges. Remember Coral mentioning to Georgie that he worked as an investment banker? To say she was stretching the truth is putting it mildly. He worked at Tindle's Department Store, in the credit department. He was stealing customers' social security numbers and opening up credit cards for himself."

Hattie presses her lips tightly. "Oh, Bizzy. Uncle Glenn's dealership is inundated with reviews that suggest buying a car from the Pitts Stop equates to having your identity stolen. Didn't something like this happen to Emmie and Leo after they bought their truck there? And the interesting part is—all of these reviews are from the last six months."

A hard moan comes from me. "It sounds as if Coral took a page out of her husband's illegal playbook once he was hauled off."

She nods. "Those Arabian horses weren't going to feed themselves. We need to talk to her."

Sherlock barks. *We need to call Jasper.*

Fish yowls up at me, *For once I agree with the hairy oaf.*

Cricket sighs. *It's no use. Once Hattie makes up her mind to do something, there's no stopping her.*

Fish twitches her whiskers. *She and Bizzy are more alike than we thought. And I'm not so sure this is a good thing.*

"What's not a good thing is someone getting away with credit fraud," I say.

Hattie nods. "Or murder. But that's not about to happen on my watch."

She takes off, and I follow on her heels.

We might just have our killer.

Someone has a lot of explaining to do when it comes to the bad wrap the dealership has been handed, and perhaps a little confessing when it comes to a certain murder, too.

CHAPTER 15

The Summer by the Sea event has blown up in size as all of Maine seemingly descends on the cove.

Ned Colton has the female masses swooning as he finishes up a set. Followed by Mayor Mackenzie Woods, who announces that the fireworks are set to begin in just a few minutes. The crowd goes so wild at the mention of pyrotechnics, you'd think a riot is taking place. And the smoke from the grills only seems to increase as the staff from the café works overtime to feed the hungry bellies in our midst.

She's over by the dessert station. Muffin barks as she and Sherlock charge that way.

We'd better hurry, Bizzy, Fish meows. **I've got a feeling she wouldn't hesitate to chop the tails off a couple of meddling mutts.**

Or curious cats, Cricket says as she sinks deeper into Hattie's arms.

Sure enough, we find Coral Shaw scooping up a heaping helping of Aunt Birdie's banana pudding before she meanders in the direction of the café.

We follow close behind and catch up with her once she pauses at the makeshift memorial of flowers just shy of the woods.

The detonation of the first firework of the night goes off overhead, and the ground feels as if it's shaking in response.

"You would be here." A twinge of rage scorches Hattie's voice.

Fish looks up at her. **And she's off the rails again.**

Fish is right, but I can't blame Hattie. She knew Uncle Glenn far better than I did. But I'm as equally charged and outraged.

Coral startles for a moment as she steps out of the shadows. Her crimson locks are pulled back, and she's wearing a stylish red checkered shirt with its collar popped up in a way my mother would approve of.

"Oh, hello, girls. You scared the living daylights out of me." A laugh bounces from her. "I almost dropped my dessert. And believe me, it's worth its weight in gold." She holds the banana pudding up for us to see.

"That it is," I tell her.

"I was just paying my respects to your uncle." Coral sighs as she glances to the flowers scattered at her feet. "Many people don't know this, but he had a big heart." *For himself. I would have cut him in on the deal. But in a twist of fate, he decided he was an honest man.*

Muffin growls up at her as Sherlock does his best to hold her back.

"Aren't we testy tonight?" Coral makes a face down at the cutie. *The little mutt never quits. Hopefully, I'll never have to see this fleabag again. I certainly don't miss her down at the dealership.*

"Coral"—I take a step in her direction—"the strangest thing was brought to my attention tonight. I just found out that the dealership has been receiving a number of bad reviews online."

The sky lights up with both an explosion of sound and color as the crowd gives a collective gasp at the sight.

Sherlock whimpers. *Let's leave now and call Jasper. He can ask her the hard questions. And if she doesn't want to answer, he's got a weapon that can make the woman change her mind.*

"Bad reviews?" Coral's fingers fumble with the pendant dangling from her necklace. "Oh, right. I think I saw those. No big deal. It was just a few disgruntled customers." She chuckles at the thought. "It drove your uncle crazy, but I told him not to worry about it. Nothing but a couple of internet trolls who opened a bunch of accounts just to harass him."

"It sounds as if he was pretty upset over it," I say.

Coral waves it off. "I offered to take care of it for him. I wrote out apologies to a few displeased customers on his behalf. In fact, he trusted me so much to do so, he signed the letters in advance." She stops cold as if she just let a dark secret slip, and she did.

"That's how you did it." Hattie closes her eyes a moment.

The letter mailed to the sheriff's department, Cricket cries out.

Sherlock barks. *She's guilty! Now let's get Jasper.*

I'm afraid it's too late for that.

Even though we don't have a confession yet, I'm guessing Coral is about to leave the state to avoid wire fraud charges—just like the ones that landed her husband behind bars.

I catch Coral's gaze. "That day we visited the dealership, you mentioned you had been separated for six months and that you were in the process of a divorce. You didn't separate in the traditional sense, did you? Your husband was taken away from you. He's in prison, isn't he?"

"What?" She takes a step back. "That's just a nasty rumor." Her eyes float to the woods as if she were plotting her escape.

"No." I shake my head at her. "That's not just a nasty rumor. Your husband, Roland Shaw, went away to prison exactly six months ago."

Hattie nods. "We did a little research. He was put away for wire fraud charges. He worked for Tindle's Department Store at the credit counter. He was busted for stealing the information from the applicants and opening up credit cards for himself."

"And that's why the dealership was getting such bad reviews—because you were replicating his evil scheme." I give a confident nod as I say it. "You weren't the top salesperson for the last six months in a row like you attested. Coral, you haven't sold a car since Christmas. The only reason you stayed at the dealership is because you were pulling the exact same scam with my uncle's customers."

"I would never do that," she pants.

"Really?" Hattie asks. "You said something at the dealership that day that made me wonder. You said it was Uncle Glenn's stubbornness that cost him his life. It's because you argued with him about not taking what he knew to the authorities, isn't it? He was too honest and stubborn to go along with your plan."

I step in close, and Fish poises herself as if she were ready to strike. "That day at the dealership, you mentioned you were living an extravagant lifestyle, house on the bluffs, Italian cars and clothes, two Arabian horses…"

Hattie nods. "You said life wouldn't be worth living if you weren't having champagne."

Coral's mouth falls open. "Look, I had no idea that's how my ex-husband was providing for us. I wasn't stealing from the dealership, if that's what you're implying."

"That's not what we're implying." I sigh. "It's exactly what we're saying. You had access to the customers' personal files at the dealership. You didn't have to sell a single car because you were doing just fine on your own. You weren't stealing from the dealership, but you needed to be there to mine them for their customers' private information. You stole their social security numbers and opened credit cards with their names on them. And you needed to silence our uncle before he turned your entire gilded world upside down."

"I didn't do this." She shakes her head as she begins to back away. "I didn't kill Glenn."

"Sure you did," I tell her. "The day you stopped off at the inn to find your sunglasses? You mentioned that you retraced your steps. You said you went to the side of the café—the wooded side of the building. You meant near the side closest to the woods—right where we're standing now. You came back here because this is where you lured Glenn before you plunged a knife into his back. If those sunglasses were found by the wrong people, you knew it could implicate you in the case."

She lifts her chin sharply. Her eyes slit to nothing as she takes us in. Her features harden. Her body stiffens, and you can see a newfound rage percolating inside her.

"Yes, I killed him." The words stream from her, heated. "I won't bother denying stealing from the customers either. I needed the money. I was about to lose everything. It was going to be a temporary means to an end. I just needed some cash to pay the bills."

"But it was easy cash, and you couldn't stop," Hattie says.

"You're right." Coral's chest pulsates as her breathing grows erratic. "I wasn't planning on killing him. You have to believe me. But he said it was the last day of my freedom. And there were so many people here that day that had a bone to pick with him. I had no choice to do what I did. Your aunt hated him more than any of us combined. I'm shocked she's still a free woman." She tosses the bowl full of pudding to the wall of the café, and it leaves a glossy splatter in its wake.

I swallow down a small laugh. "And when you saw that the sheriff's department wasn't moving quickly, you sent them that letter with my uncle's signature."

"It should have spurred them along." She shakes her head. "And it would have worked if the two of you weren't so dead set on poking around. I knew you were trouble the day you came to the dealership. I should have gone with my gut and left town that night."

"I'm so glad you didn't," I say. "Because we would never have had the privilege to turn you in to the sheriff's department."

"And you still won't." She pulls something from her purse,

and within seconds Hattie and I are staring down at an opened switchblade.

That's it! Cricket screeches as she leaps for Coral's head and misses. *Nobody holds a knife to my girl!*

Or mine! Fish roars as she jumps to the ground and inches her way up Coral's dress by way of her claws and she's ejected off just as quickly.

The grand finale begins to detonate overhead, and it sounds as if a war were breaking out around us.

Now! Sherlock barks, and both he and Muffin take a healthy bite out of her ankles.

A horrid cry comes from Coral as she thrashes wildly with that blade in Hattie's direction.

Hattie howls and pulls back her arm, only to reveal a neat crimson seam erupting over her forearm.

Fury pumps through me like never before, and I dive onto the woman, onto the cats by proxy, and soon Coral and I are wrestling it out.

"Get off me, Bizzy," she shouts. "I don't want to hurt you."

I'm about to snatch the blade from her hand when she twists into me, and before I realize what's happened, she has my back to her chest, the blade of that knife pressed firmly to my neck.

"If you're smart, you'll let me go," she whispers. "You'll never hear from me again, I promise." *I can be in Canada in three hours if I drive fast.*

Sherlock and Muffin growl as they inch closer to Coral. And both Cricket and Fish look as if they're about to pounce once again at any moment.

"You're not going anywhere," I tell her as I push her hand away, leaving me a moment to get out of her grasp.

Muffin charges and clamps down on Coral's wrist just as I turn the woman around and pin her to the ground.

We got her! Sherlock barks like mad.

"*Bizzy*," a deep voice emanates from our left, and it's Jasper.

"Over here!" Hattie jumps up and down, flagging him down with her arms.

Within moments Jasper has her cuffed, and he calls it in to the station.

Leo Granger shows up and walks Coral deeper into the shadows of the café to keep the distractions here at the cove to a minimum.

"She did it," I pant as Jasper takes me in his arms. "She confessed to killing my uncle, and she's been stealing from the customers at the dealership."

"Good work, ladies," he says as he runs his gaze over both Hattie and me. "You're both bleeding. Leo?" he shouts. "We need a medic."

One last burst of color lights up the night sky in a shower of pink stars.

"I'm bleeding?" I touch my neck and feel a warm gush against my fingertips, right before my body falls limp and the world goes black.

CHAPTER 16

*T*he next afternoon just so happens to be the very day my aunts and cousins are set to leave Cider Cove.

But before the tearful goodbyes can begin, I've called everyone down to the cove one last time for a picnic.

"To the Pahrump women." Brennan holds up a fruity concoction in one hand while holding my mother's waist with the other. "A feisty bunch if ever there was one."

Everyone gives a wild cheer in response as we hold up our drinks as well.

"And a brave bunch." Mom nods to Hattie and me. "On behalf of my sisters, we thank you girls for going the extra mile. Next time, try not to get hurt."

Hattie and I share a quick smile.

Neither of us suffered anything more than surface wounds. Hattie didn't even need stitches on her arm. And I stopped bleeding on the way to the hospital. Apparently, the thought of having a gash in my neck was enough to make me pass out.

Aunt Ruth gives us both a stern look. "There won't be a next time. Bizzy, you're married to a detective. Please let him do his job. I can't bear to worry about you."

"Bizzy doesn't believe Jasper can do his job." Camila winks over at me. "That's why she does it for him."

She's been cozying up to Henry all afternoon, but according to his body language—and his thoughts these last few days—he's not nearly as invested.

Emmie huffs over at her, "Bizzy is an independent woman with sharp investigative skills. That's what attracted Jasper to her to begin with."

"Hear, hear," Jasper says, raising his glass a little higher as we all stand at attention for the impromptu toast.

Aunt Birdie hoists her glass another inch. "I don't care who solved the mystery. I'm just glad I'm not in the pokey!"

The entire lot of us shares a laugh as we imbibe our cock-tails, or mocktails as they were, seeing that everyone is set to drive home in a bit.

Everyone breaks into their own private conversations once again with Jasper and Leo talking to Hux and Henry.

Emmie steps this way and leans toward Aunt Birdie.

"Thank you for giving me the recipe to your banana pudding. I think that little twist of yours is what makes this the best banana pudding I've ever had."

"It's my pleasure to share it with you. My bistro is too far away to cater to all these people anyhow. You certainly don't have to thank me."

I bite down on a smile. "We are thanking you," I tell her. "In fact, everyone will know just who to thank because we've decided to call it Aunt Birdie's Banana Pudding. That way, each time someone puts in an order, they'll know exactly who's responsible for the deliciousness."

"Woo-hoo!" Aunt Birdie lets out a cry of jubilation. "I'm going to be famous." She claps at the thought. "And Georgie?" She waves her over. "I've got a little surprise for you."

"You've got an ex with a barn and you need it taken care of." Georgie nods as if it were a fact. "Just give me five G's, a van with no plates, and I'll take care of the rest." She glances over at Macy. "I've got a blonde we can pin it on, and the two of us could vacation in Cabo while she takes the heat."

"Nope, no barn burning," Aunt Birdie howls with laughter. "I'm putting that brownie recipe you gave me to good use at my bistro—sans the dicey ingredients. Actually, Bizzy just gave me a great idea. I think I'll call them Georgie's Special Brownies."

"Now we're talking." Georgie claps and breaks out into a spontaneous jig. "Hear that, Blondie?" she shouts over to Macy. "I don't need your stinking candles."

Macy makes a face as she leaves Candy to run wild with the rest of the dogs. Sherlock and Muffin are running up and down the cove along with Cinnamon and Gatsby while Fish and Cricket watch, sprawled out on a wonky quilt in the sand.

"What career-killing death trap are you pulling me into now?" Macy snips at Georgie. "It's bad enough half the town is shunning my shop. I've heard rumors they're calling my inventory the candles of death. Thanks to you and your pesky potion they think my candles are combustible."

Mom steps up and snorts. "And oddly, that Passion Potion is right back to selling out again."

Georgie nods. "That's because it earned the tagline, *get ready to set the sheets on fire.*"

Aunt Birdie and Aunt Ruth roar with laughter at that one.

The dogs run up, out of breath and begging for bacon.

"All right, you mooches," Georgie says as she quickly empties her pockets of an unusual amount of bacon—which is quickly becoming typical. "You've robbed me of all my salted meat."

"I'd like to rob you, Bizzy," Aunt Birdie says with a grin. "Of one ponytail wearing pooch. If you don't mind, I'd love to adopt Muffin. I think she'd be as big of a hit with my customers as she has been with me." She bends over and scoops up the panting furball. "What do you think, kiddo? How about we agree to disagree about Glenn, and we girls form a united front in life? I'll take care of you, if you take care of me. I'll even throw in some banana pudding."

You bet! Muffin barks out her response before licking a line up Aunt Birdie's face.

"Yay!" I shout as the entire lot of us breaks out into a spontaneous applause. "I couldn't think of a better match," I say as I stroke Muffin's fluffy fur. "And now I have another reason to come up to visit the bistro."

Fish and Cricket run this way, and Hattie and I scoop them up.

I want to visit, too, Fish mewls. *And I want to visit Brambleberry Bay as well. Cricket's grandpa has an entire fleet of boats at the harbor, and Cricket says there are endless critters to catch each time she visits.*

Cricket nods. *Big, hairy critters with long tails. And there's plenty to keep us busy for hours.*

"Sounds terrifying," I say.

"But you'll come anyway?" Hattie gives a little nod as she poses the question.

"You bet," I say, bumping my hip to hers. "Brambleberry Bay, here I come."

Camila steps this way. "What's this? Paying a visit to my new home?"

My mouth falls open. "Are you moving to Brambleberry?"

She shrugs. "I may have done a quick internet search last night. Not only is it a scenic little town, but I happened to find out there's an opening at the Brambleberry Bay Country Club, and they're looking for an event coordinator."

I suck in a quick breath as I look at Hattie. "The Brambleberry Bay Country Club is very exclusive. They have an attached resort. I've worked with them in the past when my guests needed somewhere to stay up north. They're super ritzy, and their prices are three times what we charge here. The country club would be an amazing opportunity for you. Hattie, you would be perfect for the position. Not only is it in your hometown, but you're a natural at coordinating. I heard you've been doing the family reunion for years."

"It's true, I have." She tips her head as if considering it.

"Well, you can't have the job." Camila is quick to cut short Hattie's dreams of employment. "It's mine. I found it first. I'm leaving for Brambleberry first thing in the morning to interview there." *Even if they haven't asked me to yet. Of course, they're going to want me. What's not to love?*

Henry strides up looking a little pale. "Camila? Did I just hear you mention that you're heading up to Brambleberry?" *Good grief. I'd better nip this in the bud before I end up with a world-class clinger on my hands.* "Can I speak with you for a moment?"

They step away just as Jasper, Hux, and Mackenzie head over.

Mackenzie holds her bulbous belly as if it needed her assistance to keep from falling.

"Summer is over," Mackenzie snaps as if she were trying to shoo the season and its swampy weather away. *Not that I would mind. I don't like trickling with sweat in places sweat should never trickle.* "We'll start the fall festivities next week." It comes out like a command. "I'll also be coordinating all of the Halloween activities in advance, and maybe the Christmas activities as well." She takes a moment to snarl down at her belly. "Just because my body has a mind of its own doesn't mean I'm going to shirk my mayoral duties. Our busiest tourist season is coming up, and I'm going to make sure Cider Cove prospers like never before."

Emmie comes over and hugs me from behind. "Look at you, Mack," she beams. "You look ready to launch that torpedo out of you. Just a few more weeks, right?"

"Don't remind me," Mackenzie growls. "But on the bright side, once I do launch this torpedo, as you so indelicately put it, I'll not only get my body back, but I'll be back in the office the very next day if it kills me." She manufactures a smile to Hattie. "My husband is taking on the role of the homemaker."

Hux frowns over at her as if the title doesn't sit well with him. "I'm taking a paternity leave." *And if I can't find a nanny that I trust, that paternity leave might just last eighteen years. I'm not letting just anyone take my kid for the day.*

I always knew Hux would be a good father, I tell Hattie. *But he's turning out to be a great one, and the baby isn't even here yet.*

"Don't have that baby yet," Mom calls out as she makes her way over. "I'm coordinating with your mother, and we're throwing you a baby shower."

"Don't you dare," Mackenzie spits it out like a threat, and I have no doubt it is. "Huxley and I are perfectly capable of picking up a crib and a box of diapers." *How much junk does one baby need?*

Mom waves her off. *That's my grandkid in there, and I'm throwing it a party whether Mackenzie approves or not.*

If Mackenzie is about to learn anything, it's that once my mother gets an idea in her mind, she's unstoppable.

Mom looks my way. "What's going on at this place in September?"

"We have a thriller convention booked at the beginning of the month, but after that we're free."

"Block out a Saturday for me, would you?" She glances at the inn. "I guess I'd better hop on that guest list. And we'll need a cake. Emmie, you can handle that for me. I'll cover all the costs. Oh, it's going to be a great party." She takes off mumbling a laundry list of things to do.

Mackenzie scoffs. "Did she just usurp my authority? Follow me, Hux. We need to get ahold of my mother and fast before Hurricane Ree blows through my family."

A shrill cry comes from our right, and we turn to see Camila slap Henry before taking off for the parking lot.

"That ended well," Hattie says as Henry steps this way.

"It's over, I take it?" Jasper winces. "Don't take offense. Camila doesn't handle rejection well."

"I'll be okay," Henry says, rubbing his cheek.

"And so will you," I tell Hattie. "That position at the resort just opened up again. I'll call the manager and put in a good word for you if you're interested."

She's interested, Cricket yowls. *I like my Fancy Beast cat food. And I'm sorry to out you, Hattie, but she's already switched brands on me.*

Fish sucks in a breath as if it were unfathomable—and for her, it would be.

"I'm interested," Hattie says with a laugh. "And I'm interested in keeping Cricket comfortable in a culinary manner she's accustomed to. An event coordinator sounds like a dream position. And I bet I can convince them to open a lending library like you have here. It'll be a collision of passions."

"I'm so excited for you!" I hop over and hug her. "I'll go put in that call right now."

I do just that as the picnic wraps up.

And soon enough we're all in front of the inn as Jordy and Grady help load luggage into my aunts' and cousins' cars.

I offer Winnie, Neelie, and Henry a strong hug. I kiss both of my aunts on the cheeks and give Muffin a big smooch, too.

Lastly, I pull Hattie in for a hearty embrace.

"We need to stay in touch," I tell her. "Not only do we have a special bond"—I whisper—"I happen to like you a lot."

She laughs with tears in her eyes. "I'm glad we reconnected. We are never going to drift apart again. Come to Brambleberry Bay soon, and I'll take you and Jasper out to dinner. And who knows? It might even be at the exclusive Brambleberry by the Sea Resort."

"I know it will be."

Fish and Sherlock say goodbye to both Muffin and Cricket, and just like that, every last attendee of the Pahrump Family Reunion has driven off the property.

Jasper pulls me in and lands a kiss to my lips.

"A lot is happening next month," he says.

"Yup, the baby, the fall festivities, the thriller convention. I believe their tagline is *get ready to have a killer thriller good time.*"

"I meant our anniversary." He lifts a brow in amusement. "You didn't forget, did you?"

My mouth falls open. "No, I didn't forget." I wince. "Maybe just a little. How can it be a year already?"

"Time flies when you're having fun." He nuzzles his lips against my neck. "How about we head back to the cottage before you forget who I am entirely?"

"That's a good precautionary measure, seeing the trajectory I'm on. What is it we like to do back at the cottage together, anyway?" I tease.

Sherlock barks to Fish. *Here they go again. I vote we ask Bizzy to turn on the Animal Channel and crank up the volume.*

I agree, she mewls. *And I vote she feeds us an early dinner. They've been known to hole up in that room for hours when they take their special naps.*

You're right, Sherlock says. *I wonder what takes them so long to nap?*

I bet Bizzy finds it exhausting to fend off Jasper, Fish mewls. *That man can't keep his hands off of her.*

Hey. Sherlock Bones barks over at my precious kitty. *Jasper gets tired of fending her off, too.*

I giggle at that thought.

"Come on, Detective," I say, leading Jasper by the hand. "Let's go home and fend one another off for a little while."

"Is that code for something far more exciting?" he asks as we speed our way toward the cottage.

"I'll let you find out the fun way."

And we find out the fun way well into the night.

Fall is coming to Cider Cove, and not only will the weather be cool and crisp, but I'm betting we'll have a killer *thriller* good time.

RECIPE

Country Cottage Café

Aunt Birdie's Banana Pudding

*H*ello, Bizzy here! It's the dead heat of summer in Cider Cove, and Aunt Birdie has a recipe to share that will cool your jets and land your taste buds on cloud-nine, all at the same time! It's so easy, even I could make this. Well, if I was daring enough to step into the kitchen. But you should get right on this. I promise you won't be sorry. The only thing you'll be remiss about is the fact you didn't make more. And, honestly? There could never be enough. Happy eating!

INGREDIENTS
    2 cups cold milk

1 can of sweetened condensed milk (14 oz.)

I package of instant vanilla pudding (5 oz.)

1 ½ tablespoons vanilla extract

1 tub of (thawed) frozen whipped topping *Aunt Birdie prefers Cool Whip

1 package of vanilla wafers (16. oz.) *Aunt Birdie prefers Nilla Wafers.

15 sliced medium ripe bananas

DIRECTIONS

1. In a large bowl, mix pudding and milk with a hand mixer for two to three minutes until smooth and silky.

2. Stir in sweetened condensed milk until well blended.

3. Add vanilla extract and carefully fold in whipped topping.

4. In a footed glass dessert bowl (or something similar to your liking) layer wafer cookies, pudding mixture, and bananas as high up as the ingredients will allow.

5. Cover and chill in the refrigerator overnight.

Enjoy!

BOOKS BY ADDISON MOORE

Paranormal Women's Fiction

Hot Flash Homicides

Midlife in Glimmerspell

Wicked in Glimmerspell

Cozy Mysteries

Meow for Murder

An Awful Cat-titude

A Dreadful Meow-ment

A Claw-some Affair

A Haunted Hallow-whiskers

A Candy Cane Cat-astrophe

A Purr-fect Storm

A Fur-miliar Fatality

Country Cottage Mysteries

Kittyzen's Arrest

Dog Days of Murder

Santa Claws Calamity

Bow Wow Big House

Murder Bites

Felines and Fatalities

A Killer Tail

Cat Scratch Cleaver

Just Buried

Butchered After Bark

A Frightening Fangs-giving

A Christmas to Dismember

Sealed with a Hiss

A Winter Tail of Woe

Lock, Stock, and Feral

Itching for Justice

Raining Cats and Killers

Death Takes a Holiday

Copycat Killer Thriller

Happy Howl-o-ween Horror

Country Cottage Boxed Set 1

Country Cottage Boxed Set 2

Country Cottage Boxed Set 3

Murder in the Mix Mysteries

Cutie Pies and Deadly Lies

Bobbing for Bodies

Pumpkin Spice Sacrifice

Gingerbread & Deadly Dread

Seven-Layer Slayer

Red Velvet Vengeance

Bloodbaths and Banana Cake

New York Cheesecake Chaos

Lethal Lemon Bars

Macaron Massacre

Wedding Cake Carnage

Donut Disaster

Toxic Apple Turnovers

Killer Cupcakes

Pumpkin Pie Parting

Yule Log Eulogy

Pancake Panic

Sugar Cookie Slaughter

Devil's Food Cake Doom

Snickerdoodle Secrets

Strawberry Shortcake Sins

Cake Pop Casualties

Flag Cake Felonies

Peach Cobbler Confessions

Poison Apple Crisp

Spooky Spice Cake Curse

Pecan Pie Predicament

Eggnog Trifle Trouble

Waffles at the Wake

Raspberry Tart Terror

Baby Bundt Cake Confusion

Chocolate Chip Cookie Conundrum

Wicked Whoopie Pies

Key Lime Pie Perjury

Red, White, and Blueberry Muffin Murder

Honey Buns Homicide

Apple Fritter Fright

Christmas Fudge Fatality

Mystery

Little Girl Lost

Never Say Sorry

The First Wife's Secret

Romance

Just Add Mistletoe

For an extended list of books, hop over to Addison Moore's website.

ACKNOWLEDGMENTS

Thank YOU, the reader, for joining us on this adventure to Cider Cove. We hope you're enjoying the Country Cottage Mysteries as much as we are. Don't miss **Copycat Killer Thriller** coming up next. It's fall in Cider Cove!

Thank you so much from the bottom of our hearts for taking this journey with us. We cannot wait to take you back to Cider Cove!

Special thank you to the following people for taking care of this book—Kaila Eileen Turingan-Ramos, Jodie Tarleton, Margaret Lapointe, Amy Barber, and Lisa Markson. And a very big shout out to Lou Harper of Cover Affairs for designing the world's best covers.

A heartfelt thank you to Paige Maroney Smith for being so amazing in every single way.

And last, but never least, thank you to Him who sits on the throne. Worthy is the Lamb! Glory and honor and power are yours. We owe you everything, Jesus.

ABOUT THE AUTHORS

Addison Moore is a *New York Times, USA TODAY,* and *Wall Street Journal* bestselling author. Her work has been featured in *Cosmopolitan* Magazine. Previously she worked as a therapist on a locked psychiatric unit for nearly a decade. She resides on the West Coast with her husband, four wonderful children, and two dogs where she eats too much chocolate and stays up way too late. When she's not writing, she's reading. Addison's Celestra Series has been optioned for film by **20th Century Fox.**

Bellamy Bloom is a *USA TODAY* bestselling author who writes cozy mysteries filled with humor, intrigue and a touch of the supernatural. When she's not writing up a murderous storm she's snuggled by the fire with her two precious pooches, chewing down her to-be-read pile and drinking copious amounts of coffee.

Made in the USA
Columbia, SC
08 March 2025

54883219R00124